The Book of The
MACABRE

A DreamFusion Press Anthology

The ever-present macabre, a universal dance,
You cannot hide, whether you wield crossbow or lance.
Like the bones of the house in which you dwell,
Death will come, to drag your soul to hell.

~Christa Carmen

CONTENTS

The Swarm

S. Rey

The goddamn flies are relentless.

Their incessant buzzing dipping in-and-out, from ear-to-ear makes me want to put this pistol in my mouth.

The smell of death and decay has brought them from every inch of the land to this now dark and desolate place.

The place I once called my home.It is no more.

Now the stench is second in line to cause my suicide.

Focus.

I have been waiting here for hours. Listening to the sound of the silence outside my door, pistol in hand. The cable and internet had cut out soon after the first bomb was dropped. The news lasted just long enough to broadcast a grainy image of a strange looking airship—larger than anything I had ever seen. The ship dropped some sort of chemical over the capital and that was it.

Silence.

I ran outside to see people dropping all around me. In cars, walking dogs, even children on bikes. All suddenly gasping for air.

Everyone except for me.

Within moments they were all dead. Their flesh burning off their bodies as if they were drenched in hydrochloric acid. The stench hit me almost immediately. A mixture of rotting flesh and singed hair. Fearing I was next, I ran back inside.

I grabbed my pistol, barred the door, wrapped a towel around my face and waited.

To die, to fight, to run—I did not yet know.

Still, I waited.

Nothing ever came. After several hours I had decided it was time to leave.

Fucking flies! They seemed to be following me around as if they knew my death was looming. I guess whatever chemical warfare was upon us, it had no effect on them. They must have swarmed in to escape the madness just as I was running into it.

"Focus!" I yell aloud, scaring several that had settled back into their frenzied state.

I have to get out of here. Why can't I focus? I

shake my head as if I can clear the psychosis away like a breeze carries a cloud. Best not to think at all.

Instead I move.

I stop before the front door, close my eyes and listen intently.

Deafening silence is all that greets my ears. For a Saturday evening in the summer, it is profound. My hand finds the knob as I squint through the peephole and find the scene is much the same as it had been when I left it—bodies lined the streets, cars wrecked and abandoned, still smoking, in the distance.

Flies! Even more now. I see hordes of them swarming the porch just outside the door—twice the amount trolling me in my home. I fight back a primal urge rising within me to burn the whole place to the ground. Better to watch it all blaze than deal with these unremitting monsters. Why was I more worried about the flies than the chemical warfare?

Logic did not find purchase in my mind. This was the time for action. I force myself away from the door, grab what provisions I had gathered and start to re-wrap the makeshift gas mask around my face. I stop when the thought strikes me; if I was going to die of whatever is in the air I would already have met my grave. I throw the mask to the side and leave my home.

For what, I'm sure, is the last time.

The second my feet hit the grass, the stench

3

overwhelms me. What was once a grassy knoll I'd frolicked through as a young one, is now a despairing wasteland. The sweet scented flowers that once colored the earth and tainted the air were replaced with smells of death, decay and war.

I no longer recognize this land. The bodies of the ones I once knew—neighbors, friends, strangers— all dead around me. Am I doomed to walk this land forever? Am I alone? I don't know. I'm not even sure I care.

The. God. Damn. Flies.

Someone is screaming.

Is it me?

Focus.

"Fuck!" I shake my head attempting to clear the muddied images and sounds flooding my brain.

The flies. They are all around me now. Not landing, just buzzing and flying. Hovering and waiting. But for what?

"Better not to think," I remind myself and continue on my trek.

I walk for what seems like hours, but what surely can't have been more than a few minutes. I am moving slowly for a reason I do not yet know or understand. Something I again try not to think too much about. The sun has set, but the moon is nowhere to be found. The land is bathed in an eerie blue light that fills me with a sense of growing dread I try to ignore. The smell has remained unchanged, although now I have become more accustomed to its putrid odor, and other than the flies and myself, I do not see any other signs of life.

I pass the school I grew up in. Cross the cemetery my parents are buried in, but none of that matters now, and there is no hint of emotion as I navigate through these landmarks of my childhood.

Off in the distance a whimper cuts the silence, echoing throughout the valley. The cry is slight at first but increases in volume until it becomes a piercing scream that makes the hairs on the back of my neck stand on end.

It does not sound human.

Animal or alien, I must know the source. The sense of dread at the thought of what could be my impending death causes me to sweat, even in the cool, dry air, but does not slow my pace. Death does not scare me any longer. In fact, I cannot remember the last time I felt fear at all.

I can't remember...

Anything...

I begin to pick up my pace and just as soon as I do, a large shape looms in the distance. The wailing immediately stops almost as if sensing I have spotted its harbor. I begin to run, being driven forward by a primal urge without explanation.

The flies which had been trailing innocently behind me are suddenly becoming more aggressive. Darting in and out of my vision, landing on my skin...

"They're crawling in my ears!" I scream beating

my fists against my skull. Banging, scratching, anything I can to get them out.

Lightning bolts of pain shoot throughout my head. It feels like a long syringe is being stabbed deep into skull, injecting my...

My...

I can't remember.

I open my eyes. I am standing fifty feet from the looming structure, which I now discover to be a barn. My belongings are scattered about my feet, and the flies are buzzing their obnoxious tango with me—dodging back and forth but never landing. Why do I suddenly feel like they are the things my nightmares are made of? Flies had never bothered me that much before.

I continue, reluctantly, with an understanding that on some level this is all very wrong.

The flies are fading into the background now as I continue toward the front of the barn. The door is slightly ajar, however there is nothing but blackness contained within.

I quietly sneak through, dodging behind the first haystack I spot hoping I was discreet enough to not disturb any unknown residents.

There is nothing but silence as I wait.

When my breathing slows enough to hear properly, I begin to notice a faint buzzing; steadily growing in volume, but still unrecognizable. I search in my bag for a penlight...flashlight...anything. My searching becomes frantic. All logic has left me as the buzzing reverberates throughout the very core of my being. Quiet, discretion is no longer a concern. It does not matter what lurks on the other side of the darkness. Only shedding light on this ghastly sound matters now.

I am shaking as my hand finally wraps around a small penlight.

I click the button. The small area surrounding me is flooded with dim light. The very air in front of me is black and swirling like an ominous rain cloud before a devastating hurricane.

I squint my eyes trying to see more clearly, sure I must be imagining things. I'm not. I see them now—no mistake.

Flies.

Millions and millions.

Permeating the very air I breathe.

Breathe...

I can't!

The flies fill my...lungs...

Ears.

Eyes.

Flies.

Fl...

"We've swept the land. Infected them all. Roughly ninety percent perished."

"And what of the others?"

"We've sent the swarms for them. They should be turning as we speak and under our complete control within the hour."

"Collect them all now. Do not leave a single soldier behind. As you know, Xitara is only our first stop. There is a little planet in a galaxy far away I have heard speak of. Some of the finest humanoid soldiers in the Universe."

"How can such a place exist? And what is it?"

"We shall see. I think they call it Earth."

Epidemic

Douglas James Troxell

*O*ctober 9

The first thing Rachel Westman noticed when she returned home was the overwhelming silence. Since the birth of her eldest daughter, Sabrina, the house had never been that quiet—never. It was even more unsettling considering the stark contrast between the silence of her home and the screams and moans and general chaos she had escaped at the hospital. Jon and the girls should have been there. She was home earlier than normal from her shift at the hospital, but usually Jon had the girls up and eating breakfast by 7:30.

She yelled up the stairs, but no answer came in

reply.

Rachel marched into the living room and turned on the television. She needed the noise. The silence was too dense, too deep. She feared drowning in it. As soon as the screen blinked to life, she regretted her decision. Every channel was splattered with news coverage of the viral epidemic that had come to be known as Raccoon Madness due to the dark bruising that formed around the victim's eyes and the violent paranoia that followed. She hated the name; it sounded too childish, too silly a name for something so terrifying—and deadly.

The reason she needed the noise was to block out the echoes of her memory. The bruising so deep it burst blood vessels around the eyes. The guttural cries of men and women clawing at demons that did not exist. Eventually the patient's bleeding eyes went wide, their necks constricted, and their gaping mouths opened as if to say something profound. Instead of words, dark reddish bile, the color of prune juice, exploded from deep down in their souls. The end came, mercifully, soon after.

Rachel's phone rumbled in her pocket. She assumed it was Jon, but it wasn't. It was a text from another nurse, Dawn Marie. It read:

Lucky you and Stags got out when you did. We're quarantined.

Rachel felt relieved that Dawn Marie and the other nurses weren't sore at her and her friend, Jill

Steigerwalt, for abandoning the floor. She was a post-op nurse so she hadn't been anywhere near ground zero at the hospital, but then they had started using the empty rooms on the floor for overflow. Rachel had avoided that section of the hallway entirely and kept her surgical mask on, though, when it became clear that all nurses, regardless of specialty, would be recruited to assist with the infected, that's when Rachel and Stags had decided to flee. What difference could two people make in the face of a tidal wave of death?

Or at least that's what Rachel told herself.

She finally found the note when she went to make herself a cup of tea. It was stuck to the fridge with a magnet picture frame of Jon, her, and the two girls posing with a man in a giant chocolate bar costume in front of the entrance of Hershey Park. It read:

Let me just say that this was not an easy decision, but I have to do what is best for our girls. They showed clips of what is happening at the hospital. I couldn't fathom something like that happening to Sabrina or Madison. I've taken them someplace safe. I know you love us too much to stay away. The reports all say that the symptoms show up in three days. If you're still fine by the third day, place the garden gnome at the base of the driveway. Then I'll know you're okay. No matter what happens know that I love you and your girls love you. Please don't try to find us. I'm sorry.

Rachel tossed the note to the side and pulled out her phone. She frantically dialed Jon's number and immediately heard it ringing in the living room. She raced through her mental rolodex of all the possible places he might go. His parents' place in King of Prussia...The RV Park in Jersey where his college roommate spent the summers. The most likely destination was the hunting cabin in the Poconos, which would be isolated and safe. Rachel had no means of getting to any of them. Stags had driven her into work earlier that day and Jon had their only working vehicle. It was a hell of a time for the van to be in the shop.

No, the safest course of action was to stay put. What if she chose the wrong location? What if Jon and the girls returned while she was gone? What if by leaving she put herself at further risk for infection?

She struggled with the balance between her rage for Jon and her sorrow for her stolen daughters. All those times she thought Jon wasn't listening to her, she had obviously been wrong. She often complained about patients' self-denial of their own ailments and infirmities—how people refused to accept their fates. He knew she would return to the house regardless of her condition and had even had the foresight to leave his phone knowing that if he called she would assure him (whether it was true or not) that she was fine. She decided she'd be proud of him if she didn't hate him so goddamn much. He had taken her children from her—

He had stolen her children.

She marched out into the front yard and snatched the garden gnome from its usual spot in the garden by the birdbath. She set it down at the base of the driveway—and waited. Maybe he was watching. Maybe he could see. She waited outside by the smiling lawn gnome for nearly half an hour, waiting and watching. She watched the sun set on a day she wanted to forget but knew she would always remember. She planned on staying outside all night, but she was exhausted and her legs ached. Her brain pounded on the inside of her skull.

When the hollowness in the pit of her stomach became too dense to withstand any longer, she retreated back inside. She took both her and her husband's phones with her to bed. She closed her eyes, hoping and praying to wake up to the voices of her children filling the house once again.

October 10

Rachel awoke late the next morning with a bass drum in her skull. She could barely get out of bed her legs ached so badly—from all the running around the previous day. She listened for any sounds creeping up the stairs from the first floor, but silence curled up next to her like a lazy cat. She checked her phone for any messages, but there were none. None from her husband, and, strangely enough, none from anyone at the hospital with any updates or asking where she was. She tried to text Stags, but the message bounced back as undeliverable. A second text produced the same results. Apparently the phone service was down.

She struggled out of bed and descended the stairs into the silence. The house felt like it had expanded during the night, inflated by the emptiness. She considered going out to stand next to the gnome again, but her headache forced her to seek refuge on the sofa. The news coverage was all about the epidemic's spread. Things were much worse. All the area hospitals had been quarantined—no one in or out. Soldiers with guns stood behind barbed wire fences making sure no one left the hospital. Dozens of people had been killed during the night trying to breach the perimeter to rescue loved ones trapped inside.

Rachel had a brief flash of Dawn Marie and the other nurses trapped inside with corpses piled high in the corners of the rooms, the sunken eye sockets highlighted with black rings. It was starting to sink in just how close she had come to death without even realizing it was standing right next to her. She most likely would never see any of her co-workers again.

But she couldn't dwell on that. She had her own problems to deal with. Just as troubling as the question of whether or not she would ever see her family again was the question of whether or not she could forgive Jon when he did return. How could she share a bed with a man who had abandoned her, taken her children from her, and left her trapped beneath a landslide of uncertainty? She felt the lump in the pit of her stomach growing until it finally climbed up her throat and exited her mouth as a tiny gasp.

And then she cried. Because she needed to. She had wanted to the previous night, standing next to the lawn gnome, waiting. But now she needed to cry. She surrendered to her tears until they gave way to sleep where she could dream of her children's laughter.

She awoke to a scream that started in her dream and then shattered through the wall of reality. The room was dark. She thought maybe the scream came from the television, but it was off. She tried to turn it back on, but the remote was useless. There was no power. The scream pierced through the silence again. It sounded like it was coming from outside.

Rachel stumbled off the sofa and peered through the bay window in the living room. A shadow shambled through the Millers' yard across the street. Another scream erupted from the shadow. At the same time the lights blinked back to life, including the streetlight in front of the Millers' house. The shadow was suddenly illuminated, revealing Mrs. Reedus, an elderly woman who lived on the next block over, stumbling through the Millers' garden. Her eyes were sunken and blackened in the classic raccoon pattern. She swatted at an unseen apparition and screamed into the twilight. She exhibited all the classic symptoms of the fever dreams that accompanied the later stages of Raccoon Madness.

Rachel couldn't watch any longer. She turned to run up the stairs, but the entire world tilted and slammed her against the wall, knocking several pictures of her daughters to the floor. When she glanced down at the broken glass, the shattered remnants reflected back a stranger's face—pale and shallow and dark around the eyes. She crawled up the stairs to avoid that image, crawled like an animal. She didn't even make it to her bed. She surrendered to the darkness in the middle of the hallway, the screams outside echoing in the night.

October 11

Rachel woke to the sound of children's laughter. It danced up the stairs and welcomed her to the start of a new day. The carpet was stained dark brown. She had vomited at some point during the night, but it wasn't bloody—it couldn't be. The laughter called to her and she stumbled to her feet and down the stairs to greet it. But when she reached the bottom of the stairs, she found the house still empty and lifeless as a bloated corpse. She called her daughters' names, but there was no answer—not really. She tried to stop herself from peering out the bay window but failed. Mrs. Reedus lay in the Millers' garden facedown as if she fell asleep smelling the flowers. Rachel hated herself for thinking it, but she couldn't help wishing the old woman had wandered off somewhere else to die.

The floor beneath her feet seemed to undulate like ocean waves. She rode the waves into the living room and tried the television. Nothing. None of the lights worked. The microwave clock had disappeared. She hunted down her phone through blurred vision, but when she tried to call Jon, her fingers trembled so violently she kept speed-dialing Stags instead. No one picked up on any of the numbers she dialed. Then she realized her phone was dead. How could she not have noticed right away? She remembered Jon had left his phone behind. How could she have forgotten—

And then she was gone.

Rachel woke to a woman screaming in the darkness. She thought maybe Mrs. Reedus had been resurrected until she realized it was her—she was the one screaming. She tried to pick herself off the floor, but her entire body felt like one giant bruise. Everything ached and then would suddenly go numb before the feeling returned with the sensation of piercing needles. In the reflection of a family portrait—Rachel's favorite of her, Jim, and the girls on a camping weekend in the Poconos— she finally saw herself. Two dark sinkholes had appeared where her eyes once existed. She couldn't deny what was happening to her any longer.

She faded to black wondering if she would see the dawn.

October 12

Sunrise. Breaking dawn. Rachel woke in a puddle of bile and vomit so dark it looked like her shadow had melted. It was the big day—the day her family returned. Jon and Sabrina and Madison.

Somewhere she heard the rumble of a car engine. Whether it was outside or in her dreams was impossible to tell. She remembered the garden gnome, standing at the end of the driveway welcoming her family home. She knew she should remove it since it was a harbinger of death, but she couldn't even if she wanted to. Her body no longer belonged to her. Plus, it sure would be nice to see her family again—one last time.

Garden Bones

B.L. Aldrich

New England–Autumn, 1870

Grahame stared at the reeking puddle by which
Theodore, his black, lolling tongued
Newfoundland, sat idly wagging his tail, then
silently cursed the creature's unfortunately acute
bladder function.

How, he thought, does one explain to the lady of
the house, a mayor's wife no less, that his dog's
piss puddle confirms that her home is haunted?
Not merely haunted, but further possessed of a
spirit strong enough to compel the hound to mark
the very spot on which the unfortunate source of

the haunting entity expired?

Crouching so that his over thin, lanky frame folded into a knot of angles, Grahame scratched behind Theo's ears, shook his head and smiled.

"You like getting me into trouble, don't you, boy?" he said.

Theo answered with a warm snort and continued panting. The two regarded one another with eyes similarly large and brown, similarly too big for their respective faces.

"How are we supposed to earn our bread and butter if I'm known as that bloke with the damn dog who spoils good carpet?"

Theo offered no suggestions. He simply touched Grahame's chin with the tip edge of his tongue.

"I'll have no clients left, you wretch," he added before kissing the beast on the end of the nose. Theo licked him again.

With a weary sigh, Grahame took the dog's head between his hands in a gentle grip.

"Show me what you see, boy," he said.

Closing his eyes, he waited for Theo's panting to slow and for his own mind to still. When quiet had claimed them both, a slew of images drew focus out of the dark. Two people, one recognizably the mayor and a young woman whose white cap denoted her station as a housemaid. Anger had ensnared and mangled her features as she appeared to shout at the Mayor. The tight, painful nausea of desperation seized Grahame like a fist lodged under his ribcage. Suddenly, the Mayor struck out at the girl, catching her so hard across the cheek that she bounced against the wall and flopped lifeless to the ground. Grahame tightened his grip in Theo's fur, the action being the only remnant of a long since conquered urge to recoil from such violent visions.

The images faded after the mayor had stooped over the girl and cast a frantic glance around the room. Grahame released his grip on his dog and sighed as his emotion snarled intestines slowly unwound. He opened his eyes to find Theo placidly staring up at him with limp, pink tongue dangling from the corner of his mouth. With a smile, he scratched a patch of fur under Theo's chin and envied the hound his quiet indifference to the horrific visions that afflicted them both.

As he stood, a maid—this one thinner and far less attractive than the girl from the vision—rounded the corner and caught sight of Theo's puddle. She cried out in dismay.

"I'm so sorry," Grahame said. He clutched a fistful of his perpetually lank and ragged hair, which no amount of wax or grease could tame. "He...um...he does that sometimes." He giggled nervously, and patted Theo, who was now panting merrily at the maid, on the head.

"It's actually a good sign...it means your mistress' misgivings are true: there is something haunting the house..." he trailed off as the girl fixed him with a sour glare. "I'd be more than happy to clean it up for you, before Mrs. Carlyle comes back. Truly, I would."

As Grahame spoke, he watched his dog amble forward and nudge the back of the maid's hand with his nose. The glare she turned on the dog was short lived as she visibly softened and trailed her fingers through Theo's fur. With a sigh, she waved Grahame away from the mess.

"You've your business to be going about. I'll tend to this," she said.

Grahame quickly professed his gratitude, then ordered Theo out of the house.

Once he and his weak bladdered dog were installed on the porch, Grahame set to puzzling out what to do next. Now that it was clear his employer's husband had done murder in the house, he'd have to warn her about it. But first he needed proof that she would believe.

He crossed to the wall of the house, motioning for Theo to follow. Placing one palm flat to the wall's surface, he paced up and down its length, searching for some hidden psychic residue that could help him discover what had happened next.

The wall yielded nothing until he reached its edge. Flicker of panic. He touched Theo's head again and the emotion solidified into a fragment of vision flashing through his mind: the mayor bumping his shoulder against the corner and cursing, all the while stooping over the dead girl's corpse.

He dragged her, then. But where?

Grahame crouched and put his palm to the porch

boards, then leapt up and started for the yard.

"Come on boy," he called to Theo as he followed the ribbon of energy that called from the ground. He and Theo wandered the spacious gardens, ducking trees and dodging flowerbeds until they were well behind the house. They came up short before a thicket of weeds. Near the back of the weed patch, the scrub of homely greenery was noticeably taller.

The sour knot of nausea swelled under Grahame's ribs, and he took a deep, nasal breath to steady himself. This was the tricky bit. While he possessed a measure of clairvoyance (augmented by Theodore) and a decent sensitivity when he touched objects that gave off strong energies, clairsentience was his forte. An empath from birth, the emotions of other people, particularly those afflicted by traumatic circumstances, followed him whenever he went. If the girl was buried at the back of that weed patch, he would know it. He would *feel* it.

"Charming," he muttered. He glanced down at Theo. "Nothing for it then," he said, and plunged into the underbrush.

The desperation hit him first, the mayor's desperation. A reek of frightened sweat filled the air and he tasted blood in his mouth where the man must have bitten cheek or lip. His feet grew leaden and he found himself stumbling towards the weeds. He staggered and weaved until he hit his knees on a patch of soggy earth. He crawled farther forward and began to claw at the earth with his hands.

As soon as his fingers cracked the sod, his throat choked shut and a blinding terror rose to swallow the desperate panic of the mayor. He raked frantically at the dirt, driven by the fear that had seized him. When he could no longer breathe, he understood that the girl had not been dead when she hit the floor inside the house, and he was now living her terrified discovery of being buried alive.

Grahame fought against the panic, fought to breathe as he knew he was capable, but the initial lack of oxygen was already making him dizzy. Somewhere in the back of his mind he could hear Theodore barking. He tried to call out, but the feelings were too strong, and he was too close to their source. Glancing down at the pit he was digging, he caught sight of dirt caked strands of hair just before he blacked out.

❦..˙

He woke on his back, staring up at the same afternoon sky as had greeted him when he first left the house in search of the grave. Grahame coughed and sat up, only to find Theodore lying with his head rested on his dirt caked legs. The dog blinked his dark eyes at him and whimpered. Grahame smiled and scratched behind Theo's ears. As he reached for the dog, he could feel the collar of his own suit coat brushing at his ears where Theodore had dragged it up when the dog had pulled him away from the poor maid's grave.

Kissing the dog's snout, Grahame looked toward the weed patch. He could see Theo had continued digging where he had left off. With a shudder, he climbed to his feet.

Theo whined.

"Stay, boy. I'll be alright this time."

The dog gave him a resentful look, as if he'd heard the sentiment before and didn't trust it as far as he could drag it. Grahame smiled, then walked toward the weed thicket.

The emotions returned, but he willed them down this time. Breathing through his mouth to block the scents, he made it up to the place where he'd hit his knees.

At his feet was the uncovered, half decomposing head of a young woman, and her hair was capped with the filthy remains of a maid's hat.

"You're accusing my husband of murder."

Grahame sat across from Mayor Carlyle's wife, who, despite her statement addressing him, was staring at the filthy maid's cap in her hands.

"I took that from the body in your back garden, Ma'am. I'd take you to it myself, but I wouldn't dare subject a lady to such a gruesome sight."

"Poor, Sarah," she whispered. "She was an ambitious girl. A dreamer. I suppose she must have dreamed Robert might marry her and run away with her somewhere." Her voice caught. "I'm sure she never dreamed of this."

"If I were you Ma'am, I'd pack some things and

go stay with a relative. I'll send for the authorities and stay with you until they come."

The woman shuddered and laid the cap aside.

"That won't be necessary, Mr. Auden. Thank you for your help, but I no longer require your services."

He looked to his lap and gritted his teeth to stifle the urge to call her a fool. She wasn't a fool. She was a woman. A woman of privilege and position, who was likely reluctant to part with either, and would have little enough opportunity to regain them if she did. But what she failed to consider was that should she stand by this decision, she would also have to live with it. Live with the knowledge her husband had done murder, was capable of doing so again perhaps, and that the poor victim was buried out in her back garden—alone and unmarked—hidden underground without even a scrap of Christian charity.

Grahame raised his eyes to Mrs. Carlyle's. "You of course, may make any decision you choose Ma'am. I can tell you that I'll still go to the authorities, though they have little use for me and would likely take any story you concoct over mine."

Her face blanched, but Grahame pressed on. "If you do nothing, the spirit who has been haunting this house will know it. That dead girl out there has been reaching out to you for help in the only way she knows how. If you refuse her, she'll torment you for the rest of your days. People find they can live with almost anything, but an angry ghost tries the sanity in ways you could never imagine."

Reaching across to the small side table where Mrs. Carlyle had laid the filthy cap, he clutched the scrap of cloth and placed it on her lap. "I beg you, Ma'am. Please reconsider."

The two of them sat quietly for a long time before she spoke.

"You will stay with me until they come?" she asked.

Grahame smiled. "Of course, Ma'am."

Growth

Goran Sedlar

"I'm growing on you."

It was a promise. A pitch to sell our love story to a dead eye of the camera phone before the picture snaps.

"I'm growing on you."

It was a blurb of whatever kind of future we'd decide to write. Our little secret proving there was nothing special about us.

"I'm growing on you."

It was a warning that all endings are always the same.

The day before the surgery I told her the worst kind of mistake is the one you had a chance to avoid. You don't want to make the worst kind of mistake.

An untouched chocolate box was left open next to her hospital bed. Too many drugs in her body to digest all that sugar. She hadn't even bothered to read the card.

I talked to her some more. Well, I had a monologue and she listened. All attempts at guilt-tripping her into a conversation had failed. This could be our last time together, I kept lying but she just stared through the window, counting dead leaves or raindrops or whatever.

"I love you", I said finally, and she frowned discretely and rubbed her throat. The corners of her mouth were cracked and red from all the spit that she found too painful to swallow. Her face a map of sunken shadows.

Even if they stick you with dozen more tubes and wires, even if they shave off the rest of your hair, even if you lose twenty more pounds, I'd still love you.

She vomited.

Too much sugar to digest.

∴

How did we end up like this?

I find a memory of the day we had first met.

She walks inside an elevator, presses the button and turns to watch the door slowly closing. A gentle bump becomes falling. Falling with both feet firmly on the ground.

She looks like proof that life is the natural state of

things in a universe made mostly of dead matter. She looks like everything that ever existed would crawl over broken glass to warm itself under her shadow.

The tension of her standing there in front of me is so high I picture tiny electrical sparks crossing an empty space between us as I pretend I'm gonna grab her hand.

I don't.

She needs to grab me. That's how it works with me.

You need to need *me*.

.🐛

There is a memory of us at the lake.

Two lovers sharing a paddleboat. But the thing isn't moving.

She doesn't want to look at me anymore, she says.

I'm pedaling too fast, she says.

"We're gonna hit something and drown."

I call her a name that tastes worse on the way out, and only now I can see how much it blurred her vision. I never noticed it back then, she is good at hiding her emotions. Like a cat. Everything that comes out of her she buries under sand.

She stands up and tells me to go to hell. The paddleboat is gently rocking. Standing tall like this she's aware she is wearing a bathing suit that leaves sunburns on my skin. Even when she's pissed she enjoys the way she makes me feel.

I keep telling her to calm down, to keep on

paddling toward the shore. I'm too tired to get us there alone. I can't do everything by myself.

She ignores my pleas and turns toward the lake. For a while now there is no difference between the sound of my words and thousands of pots and pans rolling down the stairs. The surface of the lake looks like a cover of silence.

I reach for her hand but she slips away and dives into the cool water.

Gracefully and quietly.

Like a cat.

...

I lose myself in the memories.

Now I'm in our bathroom when she finishes her morning shower (I guess it is morning).

She leaves the bathroom, tiptoeing down the hallway, taking mental notes of all the worn clothes left where we had agreed it wouldn't be left.

When she is in front of our bedroom she stops. The door is opened, but only enough to let a fly slip through. Through a crack she sees me inside.

It isn't anything she hadn't known before. She is looking at a pathetic man going through her stuff, rummaging through her clothes, digging through her nightstand, searching for proof of his version of reality.

He stops (I stop) when her diary falls out of the drawer and I start reading it. Every now and then I pause and listen to make sure it's safe to continue, to make certain no one is about to stumble inside and catch me red-handed.

I'm such an amateur.

There is no hate in the memory. No anger. Only this choking feeling she has in her throat.

She runs back to the bathroom.

She opens the window and takes a deep breath. of us.

But it is no use.

No matter how hard she breathes there is no relief. It is as if the world doesn't have enough air for both of us.

I go through her mind searching for something beautiful, something intentionally buried...

We're back at the lake.

She never liked summers so she'd give anything for it to be fall right now. Even though her wet skin welcomes the warm air, she dreams of gold and orange and rain.

She loves the way rain makes her feel grateful.

It's been a few hours since she jumped out of the paddleboat and swam aimlessly around. But it'll be dark soon. Her defiance is exhausted. She wants to go home, and needs me to drive her there.

She finds the paddleboat stranded in the shallow. It's that same coast I begged her to reach so I should be somewhere near.

Walking barefoot through high grass feels like walking over paper-cuts. Trees are everywhere and air smells of lavender and she is thinking of a way to ask me to drive her home without losing her dignity.

And then she finds herself walking inside a dream.

Blades of grass don't cut her bare feet anymore, no, she is rustling through a carpet of dead leaves.

Everything is golden and orange and crimson and belongs to the late October and not the middle of August. A large oak tree stands tall in front of her, as big as a tree of life. Its long branches are almost naked, but there are still stubborn leaves clinging to it. Hundreds and thousands of them.

I see myself, waiting under the tree. I'm wearing a suit, but only halfway; my scrawny legs are still in swim-trunks I wore back when we were paddling. The contrast is supposed to be cute.

I hold out to her a bouquet of autumn flowers. They are all the shades of gold you can imagine.

"Where did you get these?" she asks.

"I ordered them from the other side of the world," I say.

"How did you do all this?"

"Glue and patience."

She plucks one leaf from the branch, and smells the stalk. Krazy Glue.

"That's why I was rushing, didn't know if we'll find this or everything scattered by the wind."

She turns around. She takes the miracle in one more time.

"Why?"

"Because I wanna show you nothing is impossible if we stay together."

She looks at me. And I see myself through her

eyes.

I look like something you wanna take home and put on a mantel.

Remembering the moment of your death is like remembering the moment when you fell asleep. It might have never happened, for all you know, but the results are there. Undeniable. Permanent.

For all you know.

It is difficult to peek into past lives. There's no container to store your experiences in and have them survive the journey. Dying is traveling light. Dying is leaving the table with a mouth full of aftertaste.

I know I went back to the lake.

The lake isn't really there because it's the middle of the worst winter in a decade. I'm running out of places to look for her. I've been to all the hideouts and shelters I can think of but there's no trace of her anywhere. Withdrawal symptoms are starting to kick in.

Despite the frozen lake being empty I decide to walk to the middle of its icy cover.

My mind is full of rage, abandonment and poetry.

The shore is treed with signs warning me about thin ice and deep water but I can't relate with their augury. I'm at the time of my life where I felt safe. Lazy. I'm letting myself go and showing it with a few extra pounds.

I'm as heavy as my marriage.

And then it all snaps.

Cracked ice and water colder than my wife's kisses are everywhere.

Water as aggressive and destructive as a silent treatment hates the air in my lungs. The warmth in my body. It hugs me not to greet me but to keep me.

I will never know for sure what had happened.

I only know there is a taste of mud where my mouth used to be.

From the moment I'd returned there was nothing but darkness.

Warm and slimy and terrifying. But I didn't care. I never cared. The most interesting things that happen, happen in the dark.

A lifetime of experiences were behind me, sealed in a wooden box without a lock, without even a hole to peek inside it. This is called starting from the beginning. Turning a new page. A start so fresh it smells like a baby.

The nucleus of the world in which I returned was her. And not in a way you'd think. In fact, it was more than what you could possibly think.

I heard somewhere that being where you want to be is half the happiness. The catch is where you want to be is never real.

So imagine my joy. Imagine being born somewhere you shouldn't exist.

But everything is prison after enough time.

Even, what you might call, a paradise.

My miracle was her curse.

When she found out about me, she didn't recognize her late husband. She didn't recognize the result of incredible determination, the voyager through impassable dimension, the proof of our eternal love...she considered me nothing more than a punishment.

A wake up call.

When you think about it, things hardly changed.

The fury of her heavenly body kicked in almost immediately. I could hear her blood cells screaming as they were hunting for traces of my mutation, her immune system was tearing down tissues and raiding muscles in search of my malignancy. Her cells were overheating from cytotoxic agents she used to sterilize her micro-cosmos. It was chaos.

It was self-destruction without any regard for preservation.

It was the kind of hate only a god would have.

Right now she refuses to speak to me.

What else is new?

She just keeps staring at the CT scan of her throat. She wonders what this black patch reminds her of. If this were a Rorschach test wouldn't this be eyes? Doesn't this look like a smile? Isn't this a face she sees on her larynx instead of a tumor?

Yes, yes, I keep telling her, you're getting hotter.

But she ignores me. She doesn't want to accept my voice as reality.

There is too much negativity in her. Too much grudge.

Right now she hates me. Today she doesn't want to look at me anymore.

Today.

Her hope for today is that everything goes as the doctor promised. A little bit of suffering for a lifetime of freedom.

"Oh, darling, but what if it doesn't? What if they screw up and you die?"

I know she can hear me now. It's there in her reflection. I see the horror in her eyes as her mouth gapes open and my voice comes out of her. The tumor speaks! No more pretending I'm something that can be switched off with drugs.

"Is this so bad? Is us being back together such a mistake? Is it something worth dy..."

Before I can say more she covers her mouth and turns me into muffles. I'm not giving up. After an afterlife of silence I want to scream until something dies.

Her eyes grow wide and she is blinking like an epileptic. She is stuttering.

"You..."

"Why did..."

"...you are..."

"... you ran ..."

"... suff..."

"... from..."

"... suffocating..."

"... me?"

"... me."

"See, we're finishing each other's sentences. Just like the old days."

She is coughing and trying to breathe and I count the shades of blue her faces changes to.

"I told you once that nothing is impossible if we stay together. Isn't this me proving it?"

She is now on the floor, either praying or retching.

Okay, I shout directly into her mind, take me out! Cut me out of your throat! Get rid of me! Scar your beauty so that no one will ever want you. But do you seriously think it will stop me?

She's breathing again, hungry intakes of air as if she just resurfaced from the bottom of a lake.

It'll be exactly like this every time I come back. And I'll keep coming back, over and over again.

I show her a glimpse of the future I have prepared for us. Her heart almost can't take it.

It is an avalanche of pain. Countless days spent in the hospital waiting rooms, infinite hours of chemotherapy, CT scans as numerous as cellphone pictures.

This time I returned inside your throat. Maybe next time it'll choose your eyes and you can't cut those out, can you? After that, perhaps your vagina. It'll become malignant and enlarged, begging for an amputation. Then the cancer on your tongue, then the tumor of your brain, then the growth on your lungs. You're starting to get the picture?

Your body is my paradise darling. Your flesh and blood my afterlife.

She is crying now. Tears for the wounds she won't be able to mourn after her tear ducts are removed.

"You understand now, don't you?"

Not even death can do us part.

Her brain is a diary left open.

I don't have to read it. There is an unbroken chain of whispers between her little grey cells and myself. Thousands of little voices trapped in their membranes, describing colors of blankets, touch of the skin, smell of a pillow, taste of a lipstick.

I only need to glue them all together like autumn leaves and the memory becomes three dimensional.

There.

It's the middle of the night and she tries to leave the bed. Maybe to pee, maybe to have a snack, maybe to sleep somewhere else.

I grab her hand. We're back to when I had a hand.

I pull her closer and kiss her throat.

"I'm growing on you," I say, hoping the wet touch of my lips would make her forget about the little blue continent on her skin.

It is embarrassing, intimate and painful to the touch.

It is everything you hate in a bruise.

Day Eighteen

Joshua Raines

"Is that a crater?" Stacy tucked her blonde hair behind her ears as she peered down into the hole in the earth.

Dave Evans stood on the edge and looked into the chasm. He shined his flashlight down in it as the hungry black below devoured the light. It was impossible to determine its depth.

"Looks like a sinkhole."

Big Rog, a 6'4", burly bear of a man, walked around the hole. "A sinkhole? Here?"

Dave kicked a pebble into missing earth. "Not sure what else it could be. Odd place for one, but with all the uncharted mineshafts around here, I wouldn't say it's impossible."

"Think they fell down it?" Stacy asked.

"If they came upon it at night, I'd say that was a real possibility."

Dave and his crew, volunteers with the National Forest Service, were looking for three hikers—all experienced outdoorsmen—who hadn't been heard from in three weeks. Even when they fell off the grid, they still checked in with their families. When one of their mamas hadn't heard from her son in three weeks, she put in a call to the Park Ranger, who in turn sent Dave and his crew out for a look.

"I reckon we should go down and take a peek," Dave said. "You brought the rappelling gear?" The terrain in Ouachita was, in areas, a bit treacherous.

"Yep," Big Rog said.

"Alright. Let's unload it and give it a go."

While Big Rog and Stacy set up the gear, Dave called his boss.

Les answered the call with one ring. "You find them?"

"Not sure," Dave said, "but we found a big sinkhole about ten miles from the station."

"That's a first. A little dry for a sinkhole, don't you think?"

"You'd figure, but I don't know what else it'd be. It's about thirty feet wide, and boy does it look deep. Seems too deep to be a crater, and besides, we'd have heard something if there was a meteor."

"Huh." The sound of Les taking a drag off a cigarette filled the earpiece. He exhaled. "Well, any sign of the hikers?"

"Nope, nothing, but we're going to send Stacy down the hole for a look."

"Let me send someone else out to help you."

"Nah, we're good," Dave assured. "Only take a couple of hours. And you know Stacy would be a little put off if you send someone else, anyway."

"Yeah, yeah. Well, buzz me and let me know what you find. I got that kid's mama to wait on calling the news folks until I hear back from you."

Despite the half-year drought, the air was thick with humidity, the breeze nothing more than a sewing circle rumor. The forest was quiet, as if the creatures of the woods evacuated for more hospitable climates. Only the sound of Dave and his crew broke the vacuum of silence.

After the wench was secured, Stacy put on the harness and strapped herself to the rappelling line. She tested the light atop her helmet.

Dave checked the line. "You have three hundred feet of rope. If you don't hit the bottom, we'll pull you back up."

Stacy nodded. She backed up to the hole and rappelled down.

After fifteen minutes, Stacy called up to the surface on the radio. "I'm at the bottom. I don't see anyone, but there are a few things down here: A backpack, a boot, a flashlight, an empty water bottle, and a notebook."

"What's it like down there?" Dave asked. "Is it a

mineshaft?"

"Negative. The floor is dirt, and it was solid earth on the walls on the way down. It's really just the bottom of a hole."

"Can you grab the stuff?"

"Yep, no problem," Stacy said.

After three minutes, she tugged the line and Big Rog started the wench to bring her back up. They pulled her up over the edge and then walked away from the sinkhole. Stacy set the items she found on the ground.

"Only one boot, huh?" Dave picked it up and twisted it around in his hands. "It's just so damn strange. Let's take a look in the backpack."

Stacy opened up the blue and green bag. Inside, there was nothing remarkable: a map of the area, a pack of gum, extra batteries, and a can of bug spray.

"Just normal hiking stuff," Big Rog said.

"You'd think there'd be more if they were on a long trip," Stacy said. "This is pretty light. Maybe someone tossed the stuff down there."

"Yeah, maybe," Dave added. "What's in the notebook?"

Stacy picked up the red, spiral bound book and thumbed through the pages. "Looks like a trip journal. It's about a third full."

"Well, I'm starving," Dave said. "Let's grab a few chairs and the grub and you can read it while we eat."

Dave set up the chairs. He grabbed a sandwich

and bottled water out of the cooler and handed one of each to Stacy and Big Rog. Dave took a seat and opened his sandwich. Stacy left the sandwich in her lap while she continued to read.

"Anything good?" Big Rog asked.

"Not really," Stacy said. "Just a diary of their trip."

"Care to read us a bit?" Dave asked.

"Sure," Stacy replied.

Day 11

This has been the best trip so far. The weather has been nothing short of perfect. Normally I would never be in favor of a drought, but it has kicked the August humidity in the teeth and left us with cool nights and warm, but not hot, days.

We found the Vista Trail this morning and decided to stick to it for a while. I'm getting a lot of good ideas for my article for Outdoor Life. I owe them two-thousand words when we get back to Little Rock in a couple of weeks, and I don't think I'll have any problem meeting my quota.

Carl has been pleasant so far. The past two years,

when we got about ten days in, he would get whiny and would become, quite frankly, a pain in the ass to deal with. This time, however, he has been not only helpful, but also adventurous. He even scaled a few slopes without crying about it. I'm glad to report he isn't on his period. Yet.

I don't have much else to say. I wanted to take a moment to say how pleased I am with this trip. Tomorrow, we're hoping to do a little canoeing before we get back to the trail and drive further into the forest. There's a guide there, I think his name is Dick, who would be a good interview. I'd like to get a feel for how the drought has impacted their business. It's just one of many ideas I have for my piece.

Day 12

Well, we didn't go canoeing today. The trail split on us. I guess we took the wrong path. The map didn't show the split, so it caught us a bit by surprise. Before we realized we went the wrong way, it was almost nightfall so we decided it would be best to call it a night. Besides, Carl thought today would be a good day to turn high maintenance. Old habits die hard, I suppose. When he went off to do some business, Will and I decided we wouldn't bring him next year. He's a good guy, just not someone you want to spend a couple of weeks with, especially out in the elements. I can only imagine if the weather turned south like it did two years ago.

Speaking of the weather, today started out warm and dry, but it got muggier as the day went on. Is it finally going to rain? It wouldn't be ideal, but the forest is tinder dry and the brush could use a shower or two. We've been careful with our campfires, but each time we leave one, even if we put it out properly, it still makes us a little nervous.

Interesting note: we saw a sizeable herd of deer running through the woods in the opposite direction. Strangest thing I've seen in a long time. There were probably thirty whitetails, all hauling ass past us. Luckily, they kept off the trail so we weren't in any danger. Still, if we would've been off the path, one of us might've gotten trampled. Maybe that wouldn't have been a bad thing if Carl had been the one to get stomped. I'm kidding, of course. We would have to deal with his body.

It's dusk and the sunset is beautiful. Despite the humidity, there isn't a cloud in the sky. The sun setting behind the mountains is painting the sky pink, and purple, and gold. Sometimes I wonder if I could live off the grid permanently. I'm sure I could mail articles in for income. Computers and phones aren't really necessary, are they? I'm glad I left mine at home.

Day 12 — Later

I wanted to make a quick note in the journal. We had dinner tonight, and settled into our normal evening routine of bullshitting around the campfire. After a bit, the forest got really active—more active than you would expect in the evening. It sounded like more than a few large animals exploring the grounds around us. It's not something I've ever experienced at night. Carl, of course, made more out of it than necessary. What if it's Sasquatch? Or aliens? Or witches? I told him it was probably just a mountain lion. Will and I got a good laugh out of his reaction to that.

Off to bed I go. Tomorrow we will double back on the trail and (hopefully) go canoeing. Or take a dip in the lake. I'm sweating just writing this. So much for the cool evenings.

Dave interrupted Stacy's reading. "That doesn't tell us anything."

"Little strange about the herd," Big Rog said. "And the night movements. Could be a mountain lion, but they usually don't get that close to campers. Do you think—"

Stacy cut him off. "Guys, I think this next part might explain it."

Day 13

I'm Austin Greer. I'm 29 years old. I don't have my ID. My friends are Carl Peterson, 30, and Will Hagen,

29. We are all from the Little Rock, AR. We're stuck in a hole. We've been down here for a day. Will is unconscious, but breathing. His head is caked with blood. His arm is twisted behind him. Carl isn't hurt. I came to about an hour ago. My leg is broken. It's daylight. I can see a sliver of light from the top of the hole, but it's only a sliver. I shined the flashlight up the hole. We're really far down. I don't know how we didn't die. While I have the energy, I wanted to write down what happened.

Last night, we heard a rustling. It was like what I wrote about earlier. Will woke up first and started yelling for Carl and me. Will was standing by the fire looking east. He said our gear was gone. He said he wasn't sleeping well. It's been so muggy. He heard sticks cracking. He thought it was a coon. He got up to scare it off and saw our stuff gone. I grabbed my pack and flashlight. We decided to do a quick search.

I don't know how long we walked. Will spotted something. I shined the light where he was pointing. It was Carl's pack. It was empty. Carl freaked out. There was more rustling. I pointed the flashlight at the trees. Something was there. It was tall, like a man. Will yelled at it (him?) and took off after. I yelled for Will to stop. He didn't. Carl and me ran after him. He was ahead of us. I kept my flashlight on his back. We came to a clearing. Will kept running. He grunted and disappeared. A second later I found the hole and fell down it.

I don't know what this hole is. Why is it here? It's not a mineshaft. It's just a hole. It's so high up to the top. I don't think we can get out. I'm scared. I think we might die down here. I hope someone finds us.

Dave chewed the cuticle on his thumb. "That explains how they got down there. Still doesn't explain where they are."

"This has got to be some kind of joke. There ain't no way those boys got out of *that*." Big Rog nodded towards the hole.

"You think we should call Les?" Stacy asked.

"How much more?" Dave asked.

She flipped through the red book. "Just a few more pages."

"Keep going then. I'd hate to cry wolf if this is just a prank."

Stacy nodded and continued reading.

Day 14

I took off my boot. The ankle and shin are swollen. I'm burning up. There was a full water bottle in my bag. It's half empty now. I'm still thirsty. Carl is losing it. He can't find a way up. Will woke up for a minute, but just for a minute. He won't last much longer. None of us will. I wish we had the pistol. It was in Carl's pack. If we did, we might take another way out.

Day 14 — Later

In and out of sleep. Carl heard noises. He yelled for help. Nobody responded. He thinks we are trapped down here for a reason. He might be right. Who took our stuff? I'm going to rest.

Day 15

Carl stopped talking. Will is still alive. There are bloodlines up my leg. There's an infection. I wish it would hurry. This is the definition of hell.

Day 15—Later

Carl shook me awake. He was hysterical. He said Will was gone. I told him to say a prayer. Will was lucky. He said I didn't understand. Will is gone. They took Will. I asked who "they" was. He said he didn't know. He fell asleep and woke up and Will was gone. I pulled myself up. The pain is terrible. I shined the light across the hole. Will is gone. I don't know what's going on. Am I hallucinating? Who took Will? I wish we had the pistol. Maybe I won't wake up next time I go to sleep.

Day 16

The water is gone. Carl is talking to himself. He's

saying he is next. He says they took Will and they would get him next. I asked him who took Will. He just says them. I can see the terror in Carl's face. I have to stay calm. I continue to wish for a quick death. God isn't listening. I am now paying the price for any of the bad things I've done. I'm sorry God. Show some mercy. Put an end to this hell. I'm sure Carl is sorry, too. At least I know the infection will take me soon. Carl needs more help than I do.

Day 16 — Later

Carl tried to climb out. He didn't get far. He started looking for something to kill himself. There is nothing. What happened to Will?

Day 16 — Later

It's nighttime. I can see the crescent moon at the top of the hole. I've been in and out all day. I woke up to the sound of screaming. Carl is gone. I'm next. Please God, help me.

Day 17

This will be my last entry. Either the infection will kill me today, or they will come get me. I've saved up all my energy for this last bit of writing. The flashlight is almost dead. Carl and Will are gone. I don't know who took them. I hear noises. Sometimes rustling, sometimes humming. I wake up and there's dirt on me. Who's digging? There is something else here. This was a trap. If I'm next I hope it's quick. It's so hot down here. I am in the mouth of the devil.

To my mom and dad: thank you for all your support. I know I was never the easiest kid to deal with. I hope my writing makes you proud. Find my computer and notebook. There are stories. You can sell them. It won't bring me back, but it's something.

To my brother Alec: keep playing dude. The world

needs another musician.

And to Tessa: you're the love of my life. I know I've dragged my feet. There's a box in the middle drawer of the filing cabinet. It's yours. I'm sorry it took so long. I hope you wear it for the rest of your life. You've made me the luckiest man in the world. You'll make another guy just as lucky. I love you, Little Bear.

I am putting my journal away. Napoleon once said, "There is no such thing as accident; it is fate misnamed."

Dave rubbed his sweaty palms on his jeans. "That's it?"

Stacy flipped through the rest of the notebook. "Appears so."

"This is some weird shit, boss," Big Rog said.

"Maybe it's like Rog said," Stacy uttered. "Maybe it's just a joke."

Dave nodded. "I don't know, maybe. Whatever it is, it gives me the willies. Mark the coordinates on the map. Let's blow this joint. I'll call Les on the way."

"Good idea." Big Rog stood and folded up his chair.

The crew packed up the gear as dusk settled over the forest. Joke or not, Dave would be damned if they were still there after the sun completed its journey down the horizon.

Big Rog put the wench in the back of the truck and shut the gate. "I think that's all of it."

Dave looked around the area while he wiped the sweat from his brow with his fingertips. "Oh, wait. We might want to take that with us."

He walked to where Stacy had been sitting and picked up the notebook off the ground. A folded piece of paper fell out.

"What's that?" Stacy asked.

"What's what?" Dave said.

"That." She pointed to the piece of paper at his feet.

Dave picked up the piece of paper and unfolded it:

Day 18. Join us.

"What the fuck is that?" Big Rog asked.

"I don't know," Dave said, "but let's get out of here. Now."

To their left, on the other side of the hole, the sound of underbrush being trampled filled the stagnant air. The three crewmates looked at each other, and in unspoken agreement, ran to the truck.

Despite his shaking hand, Dave was able to get the key in the ignition. He turned it, but the truck remained silent. "Shit."

"Look." Stacy pointed to the other side of the hole.

"What the hell?" Big Rog said.

Dave locked the doors. "God help us."

The wheels of the ATVs crunched across the forest floor as the rumble of motors filled the stagnant air. County Sheriff, Spencer Smith, and Ouachita National Forest Park Ranger, Les Watts, had ridden atop the ATVs for three hours looking for any sign of Dave Evans and his crew.

Spencer pointed to a break in the tree line, just to the right of the path. He turned the ATV in the direction of the break. Les followed behind. They crossed through the gap and came to a clearing in the woods. The men slowed to a stop, killing the engines on the ATVs.

"Well, there's his truck," Les said.

"Let's go take a look." Spencer got off the vehicle, took off his helmet, and set it on the seat.

They walked over to the red Dodge. In the bed was a wench and a variety of other equipment. Les tried the handle, but the door was locked. He put his face to the window and peered through the tinted glass into the cab. There were a couple of mobile phones on the seats, a wallet, and a red backpack on the floorboard.

"Huh. There's their stuff." Les shifted his face around the window. "And the keys are in the ignition."

"Odd." Spencer walked around the truck. He saw tire tracks in the dirt behind the pickup, but none in front. He knelt down and ran his fingers along the tracks. The dirt was dry and loose.

Spencer stood and brushed his hands on his pants. "Tracks behind, but none in front, so they were here and haven't left, at least not in the truck."

"Huh," Les said again. "Damndest thing."

Spencer walked into the middle of the clearing. He turned back to Les. "Say, didn't Dave tell you there was a sinkhole?"

"That's what he said."

"Well, I hate to break it to you, Les, but I don't see any hole."

Les looked around the clearing. "Neither do I."

Out of the corner of his eye, Les caught a twinkle of silver just outside the clearing. He walked over to the brush and picked up a red, spiral notebook. He brushed it off and walked over to Spencer.

"What's that?" Spencer asked.

Les thumbed through the book. "Looks like a journal of sorts."

A small, folded piece of paper fell out of the notebook. Spencer picked up the slip of paper.

"What's it say?" Les asked.

Day 20. Join us.

The Mansion
✠
Tina Parmar

Katherine forced open her eyes, but it was too dark.

I'd better go back down, the girls will be waiting for me, the party, the cake!

She pushed herself upright, noticing how badly her body ached. The stale air made her inhale greedily. She'd only lie down for a quick nap to soothe a pounding headache but the daylight had vanished.

Katherine attempted to climb out of bed but her limbs didn't follow, they just wouldn't budge. Her heart quickened its pace as a film of moisture mushroomed on her face and hands.

*Calm down, you must have just overslept...*and those pills; she'd had a drink with them. A few drinks.

She swung her legs over the side of the bed, a bit better this time. Fumbling on the bedside table, her fingers finally found the lamp. She tugged at the thin cord causing the room to flood with green light. Something wasn't quite right. Katherine noticed that the lamp was covered in a thick green velvet shade, sitting on a dark wooden carved table.

This wasn't her room!

She looked around seeing an ornate wardrobe in the corner and an old-fashioned writing desk opposite a huge mirror. Katherine stared at the creature looking back. Crawling, she dragged herself to the glass. The reflection revealed butchered, feathery hair, dirty brown, with a few streaks of piss-blonde. She slapped her face a few times, but nothing happened. Pinching her arm until it hurt, the alien room remained.

Still on all fours, she made her way toward the door. Reaching up and grasping the doorknob, she pulled it toward her; the brightness that flew in hurt her eyes. There was a huge staircase, held up by tiny demons, frozen with grotesque features and gaping mouths. As Katherine pushed herself to her feet, she looked down at the thin t-shirt and worn saggy briefs she was wearing. Returning to the fancy wardrobe, she yanked it open: there were rows and rows of exquisite dresses, jeweled, ruffled, laced...she flicked impatiently through until she found a black dress that she tore on. It fit perfectly.

When she reached the bottom of the staircase, she saw a giant front door, again with intricate monster carvings. Katherine rushed to the door and flung it open. In front of her was complete darkness. As she moved forward, feeling around with her hands; it felt as if she were in a large wooden box. Her movements became desperate and jerky, her breathing shallow. The uneven, spiky ground hurt her bare feet. She leaned forward. The front of the container gave way, making her fall to the floor.

She was in the fancy wardrobe from the room upstairs, the dresses and shoes behind her. Springing up, she fled the room and sprinted down the stairs again, yanked open the front doors for the second time, and again, found herself back in the wardrobe. Panting, she walked slowly down the stairs this time examining the front door, opening it carefully. A black hole stared back at her. She put one leg forward, keeping her weight on the back leg. Nothing happened. She groped for the wooden walls, but there was nothing, just black. She inched her other foot forward and immediately her hands felt the smooth wood of the wardrobe cavity.

Katherine left the bedroom for the fourth time, descending the stairs. Near the faux-front door was a wooden rocking chair and a tiny table with a telephone on it. Katherine stared at it. As she got closer, she saw that there were no buttons on the device. Picking up the receiver, she heard a tone.

"Hello?!"

"Hell-ooo, this is the Operator speaking, how may I help you, Sir?" Came a very nasal and high-pitched voice.

"I need the police, the police, this is an emergency!"

"Yes, one moment, Sir, I will transfer you." An immediate response nearly cut her off.

"Thank you, thank you, please hurry."

"Hell-ooo, what is your emergency please?" The voice said in a deep baritone.

"Please help me, I'm in a house, I just woke up and, and I can't get out, I don't know where I am, I should be at home, I..." She couldn't stop a sob from escaping.

"Yes, one moment, Sir, I will transfer you." The voice cut her off this time.

"Hell-ooo, this is the Operator speaking, how may I help you, Sir?" Came the same drawl.

"Hello, you just spoke to me, and the police officer just transferred me back to you! Please, I really need help to get out of this place."

"Yes, one moment, Sir, I will transfer you." Same reply, a beep and then, "Hell-ooo, what is your emergency please?"

"Hello, I just spoke to you, you transferred me back to the Operator! I don't know where I am, I think I must have accidentally fallen asleep...I think

I'm at someone's house, but I can't get out of here, and my daughter..."

She was cut off and the ringing started again, "Hell-oooo, this is the Operator speaking, how may I help you, Sir?" The recording started again.

Katherine slammed the phone down. She could hear muffled voices coming from below, getting louder and louder. She followed the racket, which was getting even louder. Going down another set of less ornate stairs she came to another door and knocked.

"Come in, Bernard," said a voice.

Katherine opened the door. In front of her was a giant snail, at least two-thirds her height, and considerably wider. It was standing in front of a tennis table—complete with a bat in hand!—and was fully clothed. He wore a shirt, tweed waistcoat and matching trousers that disappeared into his shell, topped off with a maroon bow tie. Opposite the giant mollusk was a massive toad, even more impressive than his opponent. The toad wore a pair of large black-rimmed spectacles over his bulging eyes and also gripped a table tennis bat. The snail spoke to her.

"Well, hello there Katherine, how are you feeling today?"

Why were they calling her Katherine? A glance bounced between them.

The toad's deep voice was thick with a German accent. "Hallo Kazrine! You're back. Ve vere getting vorried that you'd never vake up. Are you hung-ree?" the toad asked excitedly, his stomach jiggling up and down. The snail-man gave him a sharp look.

"Why don't you stop overloading her? Go easy Heinz, you'll just confuse her," the snail hissed.

Katherine had slumped to the carpeted floor.

"Zee Robert, I told you," said the toad. "She's getting vorse and vorse. I zink it's time to do zomething."

"It's not up to us Heinz, you know that. But you're right; she does seem to be getting worse. We need to tell Dr. Simpson."

Katherine sat upright with a jolt. She looked around; that room again, in the madhouse. How could she face another day? She scrambled out of the bed and pulled open the door. It all looked the same. She ran down the stairs and opened the front door. The black space stared back at her. She felt the smooth wood in front of her; she smashed her fists against it. She just couldn't get out. She reversed and remained in the hall. Picking up the receiver of the telephone, she listened, "Hell-ooo, this is the Operator..." Katherine slammed it back down.

Staring hard at the hall, she looked at the passageway that she hadn't seen yesterday, to the left of where she'd found the snail and his frog friend. Following it, she reached a pair of heavy metal double doors, which she yanked open. It was her very own living room at home, thank goodness.

"Mummy!" a high voice shrieked.

It was Katherine, her little Katherine!

"Mummy, mummy, what were you doing? Did you fall asleep? We wanted to cut the cake, but auntie Sarah said that we should wait for you."

Katherine stepped away from her daughter's warm little body to look at her. She saw soft yellow hair and brand-new denim dungarees with black patent buckle shoes. She closed her eyes for a moment and murmured, "I'm so glad that you are alright."

Katherine opened her eyes, ready to embrace her daughter again. She inhaled the baby shampoo, and as she put her hands down, they met with something cold, wet and slimy. Katherine's eyes snapped open. She saw that she was hugging the giant snail! He was stuffed grotesquely into a tight pink chiffon dress, with a tiara shoved over his massive head holding a fairy wand.

"Help! Please someone help me!" she shouted, running for the door, which was blocked by the clumsy snail. Katherine began slapping him. He looked frightened and hurt as he shuffled backwards into the passage.

"I'm sorry, my dear. We didn't know what was wrong with you; you just came running over to me, calling me Katherine. Are you feeling quite well?"

Katherine shuddered as she saw the toad lurking behind his companion, gawping at her, as though she were insane.

"I really don't understand what is going on here, who are you both, and where am I? Is this a dream, am I imagining this madness?"

"Vell, madnezz I certainly wouldn't call it!" Huffed the toad. "Ve are..." he squeaked under his breath as the snail poked him in the side. "Ovv Robert!"

"What Heinz means is that this is something that is quite real. You have come to visit the Mansion. You are our guest."

"What is this place, this mansion, why can't I leave? I need to get home. Wait, I must be imagining this, or dreaming it. But how? If you know what's—oh my God I'm actually talking to a snail and a frog—if you know what's going on then please help me," she pleaded.

"We can't give you any answers I'm afraid, my dear. You will have to find these things out for yourself, we really can't help you...we, we wish we could. Now." He perked up. "If it's food you're after, we can certainly tell you where to go, can't we Heinz-y?"

"Ve can, ve can! Just ask Bernard." He clapped his hands together in rapid succession. "Dr. Simpson says—"

"Heinzy, I think Katherine is going to meet Dr. Simpson, and he can tell her all about it himself, hmm," added the snail.

"Who's Dr. Simpson, what are you talking about? I woke up here today...yesterday, I don't know anymore, but I need to get home. The front door doesn't lead anywhere, just back to that room.

Can't you just tell me how to leave? Please."

The slimy pair shuffled out of the room.

Katherine followed them. "Where's this Dr. Simpson? Can he help me?" She grabbed the snail's sleeve.

"Follow us."

The snail and the toad guided her down the hallway to another room. It was like an old-fashioned smoking room, with dark green worn leather sofas and glossy mahogany tables dotted with ashtrays.

"Wait here, please," the pair said almost in unison, then left, closing the door behind them.

Katherine ran toward the drapes and flung them open: bare blank wall. Another drape, another wall. In the middle of the room was a large trolley-like metal table with a sheet draped over it. She grabbed the material, slowly lifting it. An explosion of movement—grey objects flew out in all directions. She shielded her eyes and ran back toward the door. A swarm of pigeon-like birds with human faces were flapping around the room. They were disgusting, with bloody mouths and gouged-out eyes, circling haphazardly and colliding with one another.

"Hello, Katherine," spoke a deep, smooth voice from behind her. It was coming from a tall, well-dressed man. He was slim and wearing a crisp grey suit. His eyes were watery, almost without color. He walked toward the hysterical harpy creatures and spoke at them soothingly. Gradually, they calmed down and drifted toward the table, turning into white feathers as they landed. Katherine shook her head.

"I'm sorry that they scared you, Katherine. You shouldn't be alarmed. They wouldn't have harmed you; they were just scared."

"I'm not Katherine, that's not my name, that's my daughter's name. Why does everyone keep calling me that? Who are you?"

"What would you like to be called then?" he said quite seriously.

"I don't know, that's just it, I can't remember my name! I don't know what's wrong with me, I just can't remember. I do know that my daughter's name is Katherine," she sobbed. "I don't know what's going on. Please help me? I need to get out of this place. Or wake up. I need to get to her."

"You have many questions," he said soothingly.

Katherine did feel a little calmer. "Who are you?"

"My name is Dr. Simpson. How are you feeling now?" He spoke so reassuringly.

"I feel awful, my head is hurting...I don't know how I got here. I need to get back to my daughter's party, I need to go home. I fell asleep and they are all waiting for me. Please, can't you help me get out of here?"

"I'm afraid there's nothing I can do about that at the moment."

"Look, I'll show you. I should be able to leave this place but whenever I go to the front door, it just takes me back upstairs. What's going on?"

"How can we know such things?" Dr. Simpson looked her straight in the eye. His eyes were now brown! They had changed color, Katherine was sure of it.

"I just need to get back home. How do I get out of here? How did you get here? You must have come in through a door, through something. There aren't even any windows..."

"Is that right? I must confess, I don't remember how I got here." He smiled guiltily.

"Is this some kind of drying-out facility, a hospital? Are we locked in?" she whispered.

"It's a place to come and have a rest, yes. Sometimes people are more tired than they realize."

"But I just woke up here. I'm supposed to be at my daughter's birthday party...I don't know anymore."

He reached into his pocket for a folded linen handkerchief. "I think you need to calm down, have a rest."

"I need to get home, I can't stay here."

"Well, have you tried to leave?"

"Yes, of course I've tried! Are you a doctor here?"

"Yes," he paused, considering. "That's right, a doctor." He moved to the door, "Now you'll have to excuse me Katherine, I need to see to something. Do try and rest. Heinz and Robert will take care of you." He guided her to the stairs.

Katherine ran back upstairs to the bedroom. Moving to the bed, she ducked to the ground and checked under it, shoving it toward the wall: but there was nothing, no secret door, no panels. Above her, in the ceiling, she saw an almost imperceptible square. It was directly above the bed. She tried jumping up and jabbing the square, until it finally gave way. Little blue luminous dots came flying at her face like electric fireflies. They swooshed past her head, and as she tried to duck, they hit her, stinging everywhere.

Katherine was lying on a rubbery wet floor. She pushed herself up to find her nostrils filling with fluid, but she could breathe. She heard laughter ahead of her and paddled toward the noise. In front of her was a table seating seven tiny hammerhead sharks; they were playing cards, with a pile of poker chips in the center of the table.

"Hey Bruce, that's not fair, it was my turn, what are you doing?!" Came a squeal from the tiniest player.

"Oh, cool it, Runt. I saw your hand anyway...a pile of shit."

"Not fair, Bruce. Not fair!" yelled the smallest one indignantly. "Let me have my turn."

"What are you going to do about it, you little squirt?" Bruce lifted himself off the seat.

"I'll show you!" The dwarf pup flipped over his brother's cards. The others moaned.

Bruce leaned over and head-butted his sibling making the little shark fall clean off his chair.

Still marveling that she could breathe in this

murky maternal fluid, Katherine cleared her throat. The sharks all turned to stare at her. In a flash they were beside her, biting at her skin.

"Who are you?!" came the cries. "She's a person, a real person-person!"

"Can she talk?"

She batted them away with her elbows. "Stop biting me! "

They backed up and regarded her, giggling excitedly. Bruce swam back to the poker table, nonchalantly.

"Join us person-person, we were just having a game of poker. Do you know how to play?"

"I don't want to play, thanks. Do you know where we are? Are we in the mansion?"

"What's the mansion? No, this is mummy, stupid. What did you do to get in here?" Bruce's cool response.

More giggles and nudging came from the miniature mob.

"I think I'm just having a bad dream..." Katherine mumbled.

"It must be a very bad dream." Bruce smirked. "Want a cigar?"

"Umm, no thank you. Can you help me get out of here?"

"We've never left here, dummy!" One of the others replied. "Come on guys, let's finish the game!"

"She's quite stupid, isn't she?"

The little sharks swam back and resumed their

game. Katherine started swimming back to where she'd gotten up, but there was nothing; just smooth dark pink lining covered in a mesh of pulsating blood vessels. The little hammerheads were now deep in discussion.

"So as long as mummy's motion is uniform, we will never know whether she is moving or not!" exclaimed one of the pups with the flourish of a fin.

"I don't understand, won't we feel her if she's moving?"

"Yes, Runt, if she's speeding up or slowing down, but not if she's swimming at a constant speed."

The little shark still looked perplexed. "But—"

He was cut off by a loud piercing noise, like a super-turbo vacuum cleaner. The little hammerheads were swept off their chairs as the table went flying. A sharp object was traveling toward them. The hammerheads were screaming, the noise drowned out by the awful drilling sound. Katherine clung onto the spongy wall, digging her nails in. One of the pups whooshed past her. Katherine grabbed its tail; the giant nozzle was coming right for them! She rolled them out of the vacuum's murderous path but it came back again. Her grasp went slack.

Katherine opened her eyes and knew she was in that room again. Where was the little shark? She leapt from the bed, but he was gone. There was a strong ferric smell that made her want to heave. Her t-shirt was soaked in the shark blood, which she ripped off and went to the wardrobe.

She made her way wearily down the stairs. She just wanted to go to sleep, wake up in her house and see her daughter. She would stop drinking— stop passing out. It didn't happen that often anyway. Her thoughts were interrupted by a pig walking upright across the floor wearing a chef's hat and apron.

"Ohh," he jumped. "Hhhhhello Kkkkkatherine, hhhhow aaare yyyyou?" he stammered painfully.

"Who are you?"

"Iiiiit's mmmmmeee Bbbb-Bbernard. Don't you remember me?" He looked crushed.

"No, I'm sorry, I would know if I'd met a talking pig. Please can you help me, I really need to get out of here. How do I leave?"

"Bernard?!" came a roar, and the little pig nearly fell over. "Yyyyes! Yyyyes Dr. Ssssimpson, Iiiii'm ccccc-oming!"

Katherine followed the pig as he rushed to the smoking room.

"Oh, hello there. You've woken up, how are you feeling? Bernard, have you offered our guest a refreshment, where are your manners?"

"Ooohh, Iiii'm sssso ssssorry, Kkkkatherine, wwwwould yyyou lllike a ddrink?"

"No, thank you." She walked over to Dr. Simpson, who was perched on one of the leather couches. "Look, Dr. Simpson, I don't know what I'm doing here and I really need to go home...now, so can you let me out? I don't want to be here anymore."

"You can't leave and I think you know that. Do you know why you're here?"

"I don't know! I don't know why I'm here. It's true, I do like a drink, and I know I shouldn't have had so much, but it's hard, you know, raising a child on your own."

"Look, Katherine—do you mind if I call you that? You're here to help you remember what happened. It will come to you. Now, if you'll excuse me."

"But what am I supposed to do? How am I supposed to remember what happened? Where is my daughter, do you know if she's okay? I just want to know if she's okay!"

Then he was gone.

Katherine ran out of the room, but there was no sign of the doctor. She needed to find the pig. Walking back to the front of the house, she entered the dark kitchen. There were huge pots and pans scattered around, hung from the ceiling, piled on the floor. Strands of garlic and salami were swinging like plants from the ceiling. The little pig was standing on a stool furiously chopping a mountain of onions. He looked at her, in tears.

"Bernard isn't it? Why are you crying?"

"Oohhh, I'm nnnnot ccccrying, iiiit's jjjjust tttttthe oooonion."

"Can you help me, please? I really need to get out of here, and no one will help me. Do you know how to get out? I think you do."

The pig shook his head vigorously, avoiding eye

contact with her.

"Please Bernard, I need to get to my daughter, I'm all she has. I don't even know what I'm doing here. Please."

He looked at her for a while and then put his knife down, wiping fresh tears from his face. He dismounted his stool and gestured for Katherine to follow him.

"Where are we going?"

He just pulled her along with his trotter, stopping every few seconds, listening out. Finally, they reached a musty library. There was a well in the middle of the room.

"Why is there a well here?"

Bernard simply pointed to the well. Katherine went over and peered in. The pig squeaked, "I'm sorry," and gave her a mighty shove, pushing her over the edge.

Katherine didn't have time to scream. Her body made violent contact with a hard surface, so hard that she bounced up. A hot sharp pain raced up her leg, near her ankle. There was a dazzle of light, harsh and fluorescent. She glanced at her elbow, which was bent at a foreign angle. Without warning her stomach spewed forth its contents. Her hair sponged up the pulpy mess. The stupid pig had thrown her in. Seal- like, Katherine looked up. She was in what looked like an enormous garbage chute. She heard a rustle in front of her: it was a tiny elephant the size of her hand! It looked up at her and solemnly let out a trumpet blare. The

Lilliputian beast marched around her body's outline leaving tiny white chalky prints behind and then vanished. At the same time the walls of the chute crumbled into millions of tiny pieces and the whole structure came crashing down around Katherine. She covered her face and closed her eyes.

A moment later she saw that she was surrounded by bars in some kind of cage. She was wearing a scratchy satin garment—there were feathers poking into her head. A booming voice called out.

"And now, the moment that you've all been waiting for, our magnificent, finest act of the night, The Lady in Red!" His roar echoed.

Katherine's arm was aching. Squinting, she saw huge insects, in a tent—a circus tent. They were seated surrounding her cage. There were cockroaches with binoculars, centipedes chatting away and a gruesome giant woodlouse blowing his nose.

She screamed, "Help! Help! Please help me. Please help me get out!"

"Hu-hu," came a nervous laugh. "Ladies and gentleman, I give you the Lady in Red..." He trailed off, looking at her angrily, making cutting motions across his throat.

"No, I'm serious! This is not part of the act, I really do need to get out of her, my arm is hurt!" She gestured to her elbow, looking desperately at the ringmaster, who was staring at her with his stupid handlebar mustache. A huge cover for her cage came cascading down, enveloping her in complete darkness.

"Ladies and gentleman, please accept my apologies for this unfortunate situation, there has been some equipment malfunction, but now, I give you, the troop of juggling human children, here they are, give them a big hand!"

The crowd grumbled in disapproval. "What the bloody hell is the point, do you know what I paid for my ticket? Only came here to see her with her clothes off, and there's a bloody equipment malfunction. I've a good idea to ask for my money back!"

A clanging of keys jangling and a huge earwig yanked Katherine out of the cage by her broken elbow. She screeched, "Please, please, stop, that hurts, I've hurt my arm, please!"

"You are useless, Crystal. We won't ever be hiring you again. If I were you, I'd get out of here. If Cedric finds you, he won't be happy...he won't be happy at all. You can forget about being paid for last week as well."

She looked at him dumbly.

"Taken stupid pills, have we? Drinking again? You're pathetic." He grabbed her by the shoulders and half-dragged her outside the enormous tent, where they met damp grass. It was almost completely dark. Katherine decided to start walking, she couldn't go back in.

She walked for a while, taking off the stupid heels that were digging into the soil. She needed to find the mansion, or her house, something, but she couldn't see anything. A loud piercing scream rang out, a child's scream. Katherine! Her baby! Katherine, finally. She heard the cry again and tried to follow the sound in the dark, keeping her hand out in front of her. There was a low growling noise behind her; she spun around.

It was a creature, large and low on the ground, mumbling and crying to itself. The thing was monstrous, with a reptilian face, lizard-like scales, and black eyes. It was clutching a child's severed head in its mouth. Her baby's head...Katherine's head! The monster looked up at her, but its empty eyes couldn't focus. Katherine lunged and tried to grab its face, claw out its eyes but her hands went straight through it. Slowly, the creature's face began to morph. The eyes became human, the nose took shape and became pointed and the mouth became soft. It was her own face, slick with blood!

She turned and ran, barely able to see, until her breath wouldn't come. She felt as if her chest was going to explode. She sank to the damp ground, clutching blindly for something to defend herself with. The growling creature was getting nearer. Katherine could hear its raspy breathing. It lunged for her, biting down. She screamed, trying to stab at its eyes, but as she stabbed, she saw that it was her daughter, her Katherine.

. *

Katherine awoke, deeply refreshed from the

sleep. She touched her arm—there was no pain at all. Opening her eyes, she realized that she was in the room again.

Stretching leisurely, she made the bed then left the room and walked down the stairs to the front door. As she was about to open it, she remembered the little pig, Bernard. Katherine walked down to the kitchen and knocked on the door. There was no reply, no noise, no banging or muttering. Opening the door, she called out, "Bernard?"

"Yes?" He was at the counter, cleaning the surface. He stepped down from his stool. "You look so refreshed, Miss. Katherine. Did you sleep well?"

"Bernard, I need to ask you something and you have to tell me the truth. Did you know about me, about what I had done? To—" She paused and swallowed the sob. "To my daughter?"

He looked down at his trotters. Slowly, he nodded.

"Well, I—"

"It's okay, you don't need to explain. We are just here to help you. Take care of yourself."

"Thank you. You too."

She went over and gave him a little squeeze. "Goodbye Bernard, and thank you for pushing me down the well."

Katherine returned to the front door and opened it. Sunlight flooded in, making her squint. No darkness, no wardrobe floor, she was really outside. There were no other houses, the mansion stood alone in a huge green field. Katherine walked towards the gated park ahead.

The sun warmed her and a gentle breeze floated around her. As she approached the park, she saw Dr. Simpson looking at her in the distance. He was tapping at his watch, so she quickened her pace.

The nurse on duty that evening paged the doctor to inform him that the patient's heart had finally stopped.

Dr. Simpson came into Katherine's room. "She held on for a while didn't she, Bernard?"

He nodded sadly. "I'll call the police and let them know."

The Dispatch Officer's Son

Jason Lairamore

What had once been a man strained against its bonds. Its teeth, a broken yellowing mass of raw, jagged edges, continuously snapped at us. The rotting stench oozing from it had once been enough to make even the strongest stomach lose its contents. Now though, everything smelled like that, the whole town did — maybe the whole world.

I couldn't remember ever smelling anything else.

We waited for my father, Tobias Glaus, to come take care of the creature. He had the duty of dispatch officer in our little community. He'd been at the task since the outbreak back in 1855.

Our town had been called Otter's Mill before the plague. We'd been a bit off the beaten path, north of Jamestown, in Tennessee. It'd been about a day's walk to the railroad back then. I used to love going to the station and seeing the big steam engines. Their whistle was my favorite sound. They meant things were happening.

I'd not heard a train whistle in over two years.

The fact that we were a bit rural had probably saved us from the brunt of the sickness. I can't know for sure. We'd not heard word from the outside since near the beginning.

The murmur of the gathered townsfolk announced the arrival of my father.

It was true that any of us could have dispatched the poor, trapped wretch with ease. We all carried swords. Everyone with their wits about them did. They were needed for self-defense.

A planned killing was different though.

So, we'd passed a law—one man, one sword. That was the rule for killing the trapped. And my dad was that man.

The crowd hushed and parted down the middle. Dad was a sturdily built man with gray at his temples and heavy lines on his eyes and forehead. His long trousers and waistcoat hung on his frame. His duty wore on him, we could all tell, but Dad never complained.

He pulled off his wide-brimmed, straw hat and handed it to me as he passed. I nodded to him, but he didn't meet my eye. He never met anyone's eye anymore.

"They're getting fewer and further between," he

announced as he sidled up to the ever-snapping grotesquerie. "Before long they'll have all went to dirt, where they belong."

Dad meant his little speech to be inspiring, but it had little effect on the crowd. Even the most naïve of us had developed at least a modicum of practicality over the past couple of years. We all knew that it wasn't the humans who posed the greater threat. Man was the easiest of prey. Once robbed of his wits by the sickness, he became little more than a stumbling buffoon.

The dogs and cats though, and all the wild animals out there, they were our main problem. Their lack of wits, the main attribute the infection seemed to effect, didn't greatly disable their ability to hunt.

So nobody cheered at Dad's words. They only watched, and waited for it to be done.

Killing a man, even one as far gone as this one, was not as easy as some might have thought. There was something deeply psychological in the act that was quite disturbing. And once done, it never became undone. That was why we had chosen to employ an official dispatcher. It was better to let one man carry the burden than to expect it of the masses.

The chains of the trap rattled with increased vigor as Dad approached. The slobbery snapping of the thing's motions grew to a fever pitch as Dad took his aim.

"Forgive me," he said, then swung. The

creature's head came free to land on the ground beside the already collapsing body.

His duty done, Dad turned away and walked back to return his sword of office to its place on our wall. It was another's job to bury the remains, however it was no less important, as any lingering scent of decay was sure to attract animals.

"Thank you, Lucas," Dad said to me as I handed him back his hat. His eye still did not meet mine, nor did I respond to his thanks. I only nodded and let him go on his way.

I waited as the crowd dispersed so that I might catch a glimpse of Susan Tanner. She was one of the crew on burial detail.

She wore her blue hoop skirt today. She was one of the few girls left that seemed to go through the effort of dressing up. I'd thought to ask her why she still wore such fine things given the wrecked state of affairs, but had never found the opportunity to ask such a personal question.

I hung around without being too obvious in my efforts to look at her. There were just enough people still about, talking with each other, that my immediate presence wasn't anything too out of the ordinary.

She looked up from her shoveling and smiled at me. It was enough to make me forget how to breathe. Not only was a smile a rare thing these days—something more precious than gold—but to come from Susan herself, and to have it directed at me...

A sudden realization struck. I'd have to go talk to her now. To leave after such an obvious invitation would show cowardice beyond recompense.

My legs felt heavy as they brought me closer to her. The stench of the rotting thing intensified as I neared and my stomach felt queasy, though I didn't think it was from the stink.

When I reached her, I had no clue as to what to say. My mind had completely deserted me.

"Hello, Susan," I managed to get out, though my jaw didn't seem to want to work.

"Good morning, Lucas," she replied but didn't look up from her digging. What did that mean? I thought of running away, but held on.

A small silence stretched after her words. My stomach ties itself in knots, and I started to sweat. Another crew close by were tending to the now empty trap and getting it set up once more. The chains rattled as they moved things around. Susan winced at the sound.

My brain let forth a small bubble of a memory of which to speak. I jumped on it and held on for dear life.

"I volunteer at the communal house every Tuesday and Thursday," I blurted. I had no clue why I'd started my story that way. We all did time at the communal house. We all helped raise the orphans. There were so many.

"Well, last week, while I was tucking in a young boy named, Michael…do you know Michael?"

"Yes, I know Michael," she said. I tried to pick up

some clue in her tone as to how I was doing, but I couldn't decipher anything.

"Yes, Michael. While I was tucking him in, he told me that he loved the rattling of chains. I thought it a strange thing to say, so I asked him why, and he said that the rattling meant that he was safe." Actually, Michael had said that the rattling reminded him of his mother's voice in that it made him feel safe. But I didn't say it that way. Susan had lost her mother last year to the plague.

Susan stopped her digging and faced me.

"Chain rattles are the sounds of our prison," she said. "They mean we can't leave."

I glanced around. The other diggers had heard. I could see their disapproving looks. Susan ignored them.

The chains and traps had utterly saved the entire town. Mass produced steel had been invented a few years before the plague. Otter's Mill had been lucky enough to have a pig iron mine as well as the already established coal pit. We'd just finished building our small moldable steel factory when the infection had struck. Traps had seemed such an easy answer to protect us from attack.

And mostly, it'd worked. It'd given us so much more protection than we might have had otherwise.

"I know what you mean," I said, more quietly than her.

She stared at me. I met her gaze without the smallest bit of guile. I did agree with her. The traps did keep us from leaving the town. Nobody dared to venture past our protective trap-border. It was like we were waiting for somebody to come and release us from our fear.

She nodded and smiled again, even bigger than before. My heart was near to bursting as she turned back to her work.

As I made my way home, I thought about what she'd said and how she'd said it. I'd not realized at the time of my asking that somehow my subconscious had asked just the question at just the right time to get the information I so desperately wanted.

Perhaps I could go along with my original plan, as fanciful as it still sounded to my dream-filled self. I mean, Susan and I had known each other our whole lives. And she already knew that I liked her.

Sure, it just might work.

Dad and I lived in a small two-story house just down the way from the steel plant. Every house was a two story in Otter's Mill these days. People slept upstairs, and behind very sturdy locks. It was the only way to stay alive.

I knew Dad would be home, and I knew he'd be staring at the wall thinking about the killing he'd just done. Even given my conviction concerning Susan, and my ever more certain plans to move things along, I still felt anxious to tell him of my mission.

I didn't think he'd understand.

I stopped at the door to my house to further

gather my resolve. Beside it was a small grave. Dad and I had put it there as a reminder to always be diligent, to always be careful. In the grave lay our dog, Daisy. She'd gotten infected near the beginning, when she'd bitten one of the dead as it was trying to get at me.

The plague had killed her pretty fast.

Dad had re-killed her soon after. It was an awful ordeal. After that, Dad had told me that they were going to have to kill all the dogs and cats in town, just to be safe.

He hadn't been the same since.

My hands didn't want to work right as I undid the locks, but I managed. I walked in to find Dad where I knew he'd be, staring at the wall, cup of alcohol firmly in hand.

"Dad?" My jaw ached around the words. "I'm leaving Otter's Mill. I'm going to find help."

He blinked a few times and slowly turned his head toward me.

"I'm not staying and watching you decline until there is nothing left. Something has to be done."

He was shaking his head, his red-rimmed eye locked on mine.

I felt pinned to the spot. It was the first time he'd looked at me in over a year.

"I'm going to ask Susan Tanner to go with me. I think she would like to go find help as well—"

Before the words were all the way out of my mouth Dad jumped at me. His hands were around my throat, and I was on my back. It happened so fast.

"Who do you think you are?" he growled. His face was closer than a face had ever been to mine. His eyes bore into me in red fury. "Do you know what I've done to keep you safe?"

I struggled against his grip. His hands were like iron around my neck.

"I've killed hundreds," he spat, his spittle spraying my face.

I tried to roll him. I pried at his hands to try to get a breath.

"And now you want to get yourself killed?" he screamed.

My heels dug at the hard packed dirt floor. I pushed at his face, and he smashed his head into my nose. My ears rang. I could feel blood run down my cheeks and into my mouth.

"I'm not going to let you leave."

My hands groped the ground as my vision got dark. I found a rock—the rock we used to use to prop the door in warm weather.

"I've sacrificed everything..."

I used every ounce of my strength. The rock in my hand crushed in the side of his head and I felt the bones of his skull give way.

His hands went slack around my neck as he fell to the side. I jumped up, my breath raging in and out. My throat felt like it was on fire. One look told me that my father was dead.

I had killed him.

I ran upstairs and packed all I could think to grab

then ran back down and out of the house. I reached the wagon path and turned towards Susan's house.

About halfway there I collapsed on the side of the road—I'd killed my Dad! He was never coming back. Why would Susan even think of going anywhere with me? It was no use. I didn't deserve her. I didn't deserve anything.

I turned from the wagon road and headed across an open field toward the edge of the city. I needed to get away before anybody found me out. I'd head to the railway first and see if any trains still ran.

Maybe I could hear a whistle again.

"Lucas!" I'd know that voice anywhere.

I turned toward the sound and saw Susan. She waved as she came. The group she was leaving as she headed toward me waved as well. They must have been returning home from their burial detail.

"Where are you going?" she asked once she'd reached me.

I looked her full in the face and tried to memorize everything. "I told my father I was leaving to look for help. He attacked me and I killed him."

The words felt numb to say. Susan, for some reason, didn't seem all that bothered by what I'd told her.

"Can I go with you?" she asked.

I shook my head. Was she really asking, or had I gone mad? I couldn't believe I'd heard her right. But the look in her eyes was so earnest, almost as if she were pleading.

"I'm leaving now," I said. Surely she wasn't serious.

She nodded. "Then let's go."

We started walking, me with a haphazardly packed bag over one shoulder, her wearing her pretty blue hoop dress. I didn't worry about getting her supplies. There were any number of empty houses between here and the trap line. So many people had died.

We got her outfitted and shored up my supplies as well. The whole time I thought she'd turn around and leave.

She never did.

I waited till we were past the traps and into the woods before I asked her why she'd come.

"I didn't like the fear," she said.

I thought about how much scarier it could be out here in the unknown, but didn't say anything to her. I knew what she meant. Out here there was a chance. We were doing something besides surviving.

"I always wanted to court you," I said after we'd walked a ways further. "But I didn't want the plague to mess it all up."

She looked at me sidelong and gave me a small, beautiful smile. "Don't let the plague stop you from doing what you want."

I gave her a smile back. "Never again."

Who knew, maybe we could find a place that didn't smell like rot. Perhaps we'd even find a train and hear its whistle. Whatever was out there, we'd find it.

Together.

One way or another.

The Wrong Side of an El Paso Sunrise

Chris "Irish Goat" Knodel

Shalane loved being a Texas State Trooper. She spent her time driving down Interstate 10, that barren stretch between Boerne and Ozona. There was nothing to look at, and only two places to purchase fuel. If it was clear, she might find an AM station prognosticating the Resurrection of Christ. Usually though, she opted for silence. She liked the white noise of all-weather tires on cracked concrete. Mountain cedar and rusted oil wells dotted the landscape. The road melted into a pastel horizon.

This had been her beat for seven months. The

'newbie route,' the veterans called it. And it was. Troopers prayed for new blood to inherit this desolate stretch of highway. It was ranked the worst route to patrol. Shalane did not mind. She was lucky to have gotten the job.

She joined the FBI immediately after college. Shalane struggled at the academy. She had marginal marksmanship scores, and tended to freeze when stressed. She didn't particularly excel at many tasks, except where raw, physical endurance was needed. She was tough, and those skills involving balance, speed or dexterity were her few moments to shine. She graduated from Quantico in the bottom third of her class, and was assigned to a Dallas field office.

For five years she immersed herself in work. She volunteered for various duties. She spent fourteen months monitoring the phone chatter of suspected human traffickers. After that, she began shadowing veteran agents on stakeouts and fieldwork. She had an affinity for being out on patrols, and began to loathe the office aspect of work. She was approved for a narcotics task force her sixth year, and felt she had found her niche.

She arrested Chino Cardova as a cartel mule. His brother Jose was boss of a known Mexican narcotics ring. It was a coincidence; a case of being in the wrong place at the wrong time. She and her partner were staking out a warehouse when Chino parked in an adjacent lot. Shalane challenged him, and he ran. Once stopped, she opened the trunk to find three kilos of cocaine and a sawed-off shotgun. He was smuggling blow out of Ciudad Juarez.

It was a Bureau win, and Shalane made the local papers. Her life changed with that bust. She started receiving calls. At first, it was the late-night breathers. They continued, and often escalated into threats. She often felt as if she were being followed.

She began receiving pressure at work. Her supervisor questioned the validity of the bust. Validations of search and seizure protocols were called into question. Even the chain of custody had been challenged. Her partner became distant; he didn't seem to support her claims. Shalane began to feel uneasy and distrustful. She lost faith in her department.

The trial approached, and things continued to worsen. She knew she was being watched. Her computer had been accessed, and her case notes were missing. She had no one she could trust. She feared for her safety, and began carrying her service pistol during off-duty hours.

Then she was attacked at home. Shalane entered her apartment late one evening. She spent another day answering questions about the Cardova case. She was tired, and simply tossed her keys onto the table. She walked down the hall, dropping clothing as she went. She wanted to stand in the shower and feel the warm water cascade over her body.

A man stepped out from the shadows. He wore a

silk stocking over his head and was holding a knife. He lunged towards Shalane, attempting to stab her torso. She rolled with the thrust, feeling the cold steel tear layers of skin away from her ribcage. Everything above her waist was bare. All that remained was her belt, slacks and her 9mm pistol. She pulled it from the small of her back and fired three rounds at the intruder. The first two went wide and ripped through the corridor drywall. The third embedded in the man's chest, just left of center mass. He spit crimson sputum and dropped to his knees. He stared at her in disbelief, as he flopped limply at her bare feet.

She threw on a shirt and called 911. Then, she collapsed in a futon, and drew her legs into a tight fetal position. She cried until she heard the responders. The corpse was identified as a cartel hit man. She should have been dead.

Shalane took a week of administrative leave. She spoke with the Bureau psychiatrist about the shooting, and felt comfortable enough to bring up her departmental concerns. She mentioned the pressure and interrogations surrounding the Cardova case. As her story shifted from the shooting, the doctor closed his notebook and nodded. She confessed her fear that someone within the FBI was on the cartel's payroll. She felt that the trial was being sabotaged, and that her life might still be in danger. He documented her allegations, but Shalane left feeling unsettled.

The next day, she was suspended. Her cases

were given to her partner, and she was asked to turn in her badge and gun. Internal Affairs was investigating the shooting, and a claim of wrongful death had been launched. Shalane complied, but after two days gave her notice. She'd had enough. She was out.

She heard on the news that the Cardova case was dropped due to procedural negligence. She called in a favor with the Texas State Troopers. She relocated to Boerne, thirty miles north of San Antonio. She severed all ties, and did not leave a forwarding address. Shalane started her life over.

She was well received by the Troopers. Most were veterans who got their start in the military or other law enforcement agencies. Shalane worked hard, but kept to herself. She rarely shared personal information and never joined her colleagues for social engagements. She had become jaded. She also became lonely.

Shalane was pretty, but found her photographic attributes negated by her 6'2" height. Since seventh grade, her long legs had blocked every potential relationship. Auburn hair, green eyes and a pouty smile seemed to work for shorter girls. She couldn't understand why she couldn't hold on to a boyfriend.

As far as dating at work, that possibility ended after her suspension at the FBI. She hadn't been laid since her third year in the Bureau, and even then it was awkward and forced. Besides, she had dated agents, and found that their cases, their careers or their wives always caused problems. Her Trooper colleagues were all twenty years her senior, or were angry women. That left the civilian sector, but she wasn't a part of that world.

When not in uniform, Shalane was shy, unsure and habitually hated herself. Her confidence was little more than applied mimicry of people who found themselves worthwhile. She recreated assertive facial features, mannerisms and verbal cues during everyday life. To her, this faux persona radiated a confidence that inspired respect; to most, she seemed a pretentious bitch.

As part of her new start, Shalane re-discovered running. With a blazing 2:41 marathon personal best, she could easily win her age group at most events. In fact, outside of the Big Six—Boston, New York, Chicago, Berlin, London and Tokyo— she had a good chance of placing overall female. Her long legs and torso gave her an incredible edge, and whether road or trail, she would cruise past rivals at an ever-increasing pace. Afterwards, she'd have nothing left. It was her escape; her ever important other life.

She tried to date within the running community. She joined several online forums and even the local running club. Her schedule constantly pulled her out of anything close to regular attendance, but she met several men who seemed compatible. Three immediately bailed at the height difference, while one balked at her occupation. The last candidate, Bailey, only seemed to be wary of her sub-six minute/mile pace. She adjusted that accordingly.

Bailey was a chemist of some sort; Shalane only knew that he worked at the university. He'd occasionally complain about tenure hearings or lecturing to first-year students. He was divorced with no kids, and owned a small boat along the Gulf Coast. He, too, ran as an outlet.

He seemed courteous, attentive and most importantly—interested. Shalane realized how lonely she had become. She only hoped her growing need for human interaction hadn't made her desperate. Bailey seemed nice, so she ran with him for a couple of weeks.

After a full month of increasingly longer distances, Bailey asked if she'd like to have dinner. It was surprisingly pleasant. The evening ended with late- night coffee and a passionate kiss on her porch swing. They met regularly for lunches, and after the third evening dinner, she gave herself to him. She was happy.

Weeks passed. One evening in bed, Bailey suggested an outing. He spun it as a 'romantic getaway to the New Mexico Marathon.' Shalane was free for the long weekend, and saw no reason not to give it a try. She agreed, and quickly registered for the event. The race was only three weeks away. She left her schedule and contact information at the Trooper desk, and packed her gear. She was surprised at how excited she was.

Bailey pulled up in front of her flat and gave two

staccato taps to his horn. She ran down with a carry-on bag and a backpack stuffed with running gear. His duffel seemed less full and much more casually packed. She made a quick mental note not to let her OCD show during this initial outing. Bailey popped in a compilation CD he had burned for the drive, and let down the convertible top. They hit the road as the morning mist burned off the pavement. Shalane was having a blast.

About ninety minutes shy of their destination, a large truck veered in front of Bailey's BMW, almost clipping the driver side fender. He was cruising about eight MPH above the legal limit in the slow lane, so there really wasn't a reason for the truck to veer so aggressively. Shalane looked both forward and back, but saw no other vehicles. Bailey stuck his arm straight up and gave the truck the middle finger. It immediately slammed on the brakes. Bailey had to spin the wheel to the left to avoid collision.

The BMW shot across the fast lane and slid diagonally into the median, kicking up rocks and dried scrub. Seconds passed, as a thick cloud of yellow dust settled over the car. The truck pulled slowly over next to them, and an open bottle was tossed into the back seat. Dip juice and warm urine covered everything. The scent spread, as the gear and fabric absorbed the pungent liquid. Laughing, the truck driver pulled away...but not before a hairy arm stretched out and gave its own version of the finger.

Bailey came unhinged. He lunged at the passenger's dash compartment and was jerked back by his own seatbelt strap. Twice more he tried to lean forward, but kept being restrained. His temples were throbbing; he couldn't speak. Froth pooled at the corners of his lips. Shalane opened the glove box for him—he snatched out a pistol. He threw off his seatbelt and jumped out of the car, then knelt down and shot four rounds at the truck. Even at a quarter- mile, she could see the taillights engage. Bailey stood there, close to hyperventilating. Not one round had hit its target. The pistol hung limply, and empty, at his side.

Shalane saw the truck roll to a stop, cut across the median and drive past them heading back east. It disappeared into the hazy waves on the shimmering horizon. *Probably going for the local PD.*

She climbed out of the car and walked over to Bailey. He had not moved since firing the final round. His breathing regulated and he wasn't quite as discolored, but he was far from calm. Shalane found herself wary of engaging him, but at least wanted him disarmed. She could see that the weapon was empty, but knew police involvement was probable, and having the gun brandished, empty or not, could lead to larger issues.

She moved toward him and held out her hand. He embraced her and began sobbing. She closed her eyes. Mentally, she recited phrases that might coax the gun from him. She opted for an authoritative request, but never got the chance. She opened her eyes to the sound of a maxed engine. She only had seconds to dive sideways to avoid being hit. The impact was piercing. They were showered with debris.

The truck rammed Bailey's BMW at eighty miles per hour. The entire vehicle seemed to scatter into its respective parts. Shalane was hit by glass, a sharp piece of steel and was grazed by a tire rim. Bailey landed in a patch of rock and cacti. He seemed moderately injured, but in a lot of pain. His most visible injury was a long gash across his face and neck. The truck didn't seem phased by the impact—its grill guard having taken the worst of the collision. It drove on for several minutes before coasting to a stop in the westbound lane.

Shalane needed a moment to regroup. The truck was still sitting a good quarter-mile away, but the sun was beginning to set behind it, so visibility was poor. Bailey simply remained in the cacti, softly gasping and staring skyward in a state of shock. She saw her backpack, and quickly grabbed it. Her flip-flops had been kicked off during the drive, and were now lost. She slid on her running sandals and dumped the bag's contents on the ground. Her cellphone was soaked, and inoperable. Everything reeked of urine.

They had no transportation and there were hostiles. She started scrounging around for the bottled waters Bailey had packed. She found three in the vehicular debris that weren't smashed or leaking. As she poured these into her hydration vest, she heard an engine rev again. The truck made a slow U-turn against traffic...it was returning. She fastened her vest, stuffed some edible fuel and sunscreen into the front pockets, and made sure she had her wallet. She ran over to get Bailey.

He wasn't breathing, and his skin was cooling. Shalane rolled him over to see a connecting rod bifurcating his lower back. She saw that it was embedded in his kidney. His body had probably shielded it from piercing her. None of the blood was visible; it had made its way into the sand.

Bailey was dead. Shalane cast a quick glance in the direction of the approaching truck. It was still moving slowly, cautiously. She crouched to mask her movements in the available scrub. The interstate shoulders were flanked with barbed wire, and with the orientation of the setting sun, Shalane was well within visibility.

She surveyed the surrounding terrain; she saw a few distant oil wells and a single shack on the horizon. To reach it, she'd have to cross two lanes of Interstate ten, get through the barbed wire, and cross several miles of open terrain. But more importantly, why were these men coming back? What would they do? Hopefully, seeing Bailey's corpse would sober them into a retreat, or simply panic them away. Maybe they'd flee the scene.

The truck rolled fifteen feet short of Bailey's body and stopped. Two shadows stepped down from the truck cab and knelt down to look at his body. One checked his pulse, while the other leaned down and grabbed Bailey's wallet. They nodded to each other. The driver leaned into the cab and removed a long shadow. Although obscured by the setting sun, his actions were unmistakable. She watched as the man aimed the rifle and fired into the corpse. Then he fired a second shot. As the staccato echoes faded, both figures turned in Shalane's direction and motioned for her to approach them. She wasn't sure they could see her, so she stayed perfectly still. They waited a minute, shrugged to each other, and climbed back into the truck.

The engine roared to life, and the truck spun its tires back onto the interstate. It headed west, in the direction they had initially been traveling. Shalane found herself letting out a long, pronounced exhalation. She returned to Bailey's body and closed his eyes, covered him with a piece of gnarled metal, and crossed herself in a silent prayer.

She was miles from anywhere—she would have to cover the distance on foot. The sun stayed ahead of her as she began a slow run. The heat was beginning to break, although the highway pavement still held its radiant cache. Shalane had debated backtracking, but knew it was at least eighty miles to the last settlement, where they'd gotten fuel. Ahead was the unknown, but Bailey seemed to think they were closing in on the New

Mexico border. That would put them near El Paso.

She kept a steady, although slow pace for the first two hours; then she began an interval system of fifteen minutes walking and forty-five minutes running. Twice, she stopped to sip what little water she carried and gnawed on a Slim Jim. In many ways, this was not unlike her ultra-distance training runs. She would often do five to six hours at a time to build her endurance. Thinking of it that way made the night a bit bearable. Shalane knew there was a strong possibility that whoever killed Bailey would return for her. She was a witness; she was a loose end. So she kept her eyes on the highway horizon, and anytime she saw approaching lights, found cover.

She only slept for ninety minutes, and woke just before dawn. She was confused, damp and cold. After a sip of water and a salt packet, she composed herself, relieved herself and tried again to get her cellphone to power up. It was still dead. She tossed it into a patch of sotol, and resumed her trek. The sun began to backlight her path, and helped warm and dry the dew from her clothes. She had discovered during the latter parts of the night that she could lose herself completely in her run. She simply dialed in a pace and let her body take control. It was almost like sleeping on her feet.

She continued in a semi-conscious state through the morning hours until traffic began to pick up. She began to allow the hope of finding help enter her mind. The increase in cars seemed more than a casual spike due to rush hour; she began to convince herself that she was nearing El Paso. She estimated total time and pace to hash out a rough figure of distance traveled. As best she could determine, she'd covered close to sixty miles, give or take. Bailey thought the border was just over an hour where they were attacked. She had to be close.

She strained to see into the shimmering distance. She thought she saw an overpass, or a structure of some kind. She picked up her pace. As she neared the object, she could see it was a disabled vehicle—a sedan of some type. She began a rejuvenated rush toward the car. Maybe the owner had a cellphone. Maybe she could get a ride into town. To help...maybe...

A powerful blow stopped Shalane completely. Only then did the sharp *CRACK* of the rifle catch up with her. She stood, confused, then looked down to see a gaping wound in the center of her stomach. She collapsed onto the pavement, and through her horizontal vision, saw the sedan backing up to her. The man who shot Bailey stepped out and knelt down beside her. He smiled and lit a cigarette. After several contemplative drags, he dropped the cigarette and stood up. He crushed it under his wingtips and slipped a .45 out from behind his back. He aimed the pistol at Shalane's head and fired twice.

As the sedan drove away, a passenger spoke into

a cell phone.

"Tell Cardova it's done. Oh, and let him know he was right...that bitch sure could run."

Virus

Sara E. Lundberg

A girl walks into the bathroom right after me. We each pick a stall and lock ourselves in. I sit down and start to do my thing when I hear her make a phone call.

All else aside, to me, bathroom etiquette does not allow for cell phone usage. I think it's one of the most annoying, most disgusting things a person can do. It's bad enough this girl probably conducts her business while doing her business in the comfort of her own home, but she is in a public restroom and has now brought my business into it. I sit there uncomfortably, trying to be as quiet as I can.

Of course, I can't help but overhear her

conversation. There is only a partial wall of metal between us, and I can see her feet. Not to mention her voice echoing off of the walls. Why is it that bathrooms echo so much? Nothing quite like the echoing sounds of urination.

She starts to tell a story to the person on the other end of the phone. I wonder if the other person can tell she's in a bathroom.

"So, I had a math test today," she begins. "I was just sitting there in the testing room when there's this guy that falls on the floor and starts throwing up." She pauses for a second, waiting for a response. "Yeah at first I had no idea what was going on, but I look over and see this guy on the floor.' Again, a pause. "Yeah I think the TA called the Health Clinic or whatever, there were all these people crowded around him. They moved us to another room to finish our tests." She flushes and makes her way to the sinks to wash her hands. I sit, frozen to the spot, morbidly listening to her tale.

I think about the classrooms upstairs, the giant testing room for all the math classes—the anxiety I felt back when I had to take tests in that room. What a pain to be interrupted like that. I always wanted in and out as quickly as I could. I am abysmal at math.

Once she is gone, I finish what I am doing and head back down the hall to work. I was a student at this University long ago, and now I work here, unable to escape.

Ashley, the student assistant for our office, sits at the front counter popping her bubblegum and browsing Facebook.

"I hate it when people talk on their cell phones in the bathroom," I say with disgust.

She glances at me and shrugs. "Yeah, pretty gross."

"That aside, she did tell an interesting story about a guy who started throwing up in the middle of a math test in the testing room upstairs."

"Wow," she says, sounding unimpressed.

I shrug and go back to my office, letting the matter drop.

But I have this mildly creeped out feeling I can't get rid of.

An hour or so later, a student comes in with a friend and I overhear him telling a story similar to the one I'd been forced to hear in the bathroom earlier. I think he must have been in the same class, but it wasn't a math test he was taking, it was English class. They don't teach English in this building. That's all he says on the matter, though, and Ashley helps him fill out a form to drop a class.

I think about the email the University sent out a month or so ago warning us that there had been many more cases of influenza this season than any other season, but I don't worry about it.

Or at least I don't worry until Ashley falls to the floor and starts vomiting like she's possessed an hour or so later. Our office manager, Ann, rushes out of her office and kneels at her side.

"Call the Health Center, quickly," she tells me.

I do, but I can't get through. I try three times, then when I finally get someone they put me on hold. I sit on hold for ten minutes.

While I'm waiting on hold, my cell phone chirps that I have a text message. Ann's phone buzzes and Ashley's phone beeps within moments of mine. The University's new emergency text messaging system. I open up my phone and feel the blood drain from my face.

"The University is now under quarantine. Nobody may enter or leave campus. Highly contagious influenza virus traveling quickly from person to person, believed to be contracted through the air. Please stay where you are and remain calm while awaiting further instructions."

I sit nervously in my office, wagging my knees back and forth, still on hold with the Health Center.

Someone finally picks up. When I tell them about Ashley, she replies curtly, "We just can't do anything for her right now, we are overwhelmed with the same cases all over campus. We will get to her when we can, but for now do what you can to make sure she doesn't choke on her own vomit."

That's it.

I look out into the other room and see Ashley still on the floor, convulsing.

"Keep her on her side so she doesn't choke," I tell Ann.

I pace my office, unable to work, unable to sit

still. I feel trapped. I look out the window—nobody is walking around. People sit huddled together in clumps watching other people as they lay on their sides and dry heave or vomit.

An hour passes and then two. I pace, I chew my nails, I check the internet for news. I poke my head out of my office to check on Ashley. She is barely moving now, rocking back and forth, weakly attempting to throw up, although there is nothing left inside of her.

Not able to think of anything else to do, I call the Health Clinic again to see if they are any closer to sending help. It rings forever, and when I am about to give up, someone answers.

"Are you sending help?" the voice asks desperately.

"What?" I say, alarmed.

"Who is this," she barks.

I tell her who I am and that we are still waiting for help.

"We are all waiting for help but nobody is coming. People are dying and nobody is coming. We are all going to die. None of us can leave and we are all going to die!" she screams hysterically.

I hang up the phone calmly and look out into the other room. It feels like I am looking down a long hallway. I see Ashley still on the floor, and sure enough, she is dead. She is unmoving and her eyes are opened, empty and glazed. There is vomit crusted at the sides of her mouth and her body is frozen in her last painful convulsion.

I don't see Ann.

"Ann?" I call, trying to keep the panic from my voice. I have never seen a dead body. I take a handful of tissues from my desk and press them against my face to avoid breathing in whatever killed Ashley.

It's too late, it's too late, a voice screams inside my head.

I go to my office door and press myself against the wall, inching my way towards Ann's office.

"Ann," I call again, voice muffled by tissue. Still no answer. I peek around the corner of her office. She is lying on the floor next to a puddle of vomit, phone in her hand, dry heaving.

I run. Out the office door, down the hall, and to the exit of the building. My face is still pressed into the tissue. I hope the flimsy paper can somehow save me. Too late, too late. It was too late in the bathroom with the girl on her cell phone. I think of that enclosed room, half naked, sharing the air that she filled with her breath as she told the story of the vomiting boy. Why didn't they quarantine that whole class right away? I am shaking with anger and fear.

I dash outside and it looks how I imagine a battlefield would. Bodies lay in convulsing heaps or unmoving heaps, the stench of vomit and death overpowering through my now damp paper shield. It is as if I am the only one left alive.

I feel the urge to vomit and hope it's not because of the virus. It feels like a natural reaction, though. I clamp my hand harder on my face and press my eyes closed to shut out the scene until I get my stomach under control.

"Live!" I yell. "Escape! Survive! Run!" So I do. I take off like I'm running a one hundred meter dash. I sidestep around bodies or leap over them, ignoring the fact that they are bodies, seeing them as hurdles instead of people who were living and breathing an hour ago. I dart onward, towards the edge of campus.

They have set up a perimeter. There are men in fatigues and masks holding rifles. Tanks block traffic coming in and out.

As if a wall of masked men and tanks can stop the air from escaping. I keep running. They are shouting at me, but I don't understand the words. As I get closer, they raise their guns, their body language conveying what words will not. That is when I notice the other bodies. These are different. They are still curled in on themselves, but there is one big difference. Blood.

I stop, panting heavily. My tissue has dissolved into nothing so I let it drop. I gaze hard at the troops training their guns at me and look back the way I came. Death on either side. Is it a good day to die?

Not really. But I do have a choice. I stare at the prison that was my school, my work, my life for almost a decade. I turn slowly forward, facing the men head on.

I smile at them and start to run.

Their expressions don't change, but I am close enough to see them squeeze the triggers. I feel a ripping pain in my side, but I keep smiling, gritting my teeth through the pain, and keep running. The next one I barely feel, just a tugging sensation. I laugh. It will never get me. I don't know if I am running anymore but I feel like I am still moving— not curled in a ball throwing up everything inside of me including my soul.

The Machine

A.F. Munson

Lamplight flickered on the brick walls of the old fallout shelter in the basement of Henry's home. Shadows dipped and danced in the light.

Now what was I doing again? Oh, yes. That's right. I was making the final adjustments on the machine so it's ready for tomorrow night.

He looked around the makeshift laboratory. *Did I make this mess?*

Tools were knocked over and papers scattered on the table and floor. His head was pounding terribly.

"That hag of a wife has been in here going through my things again." He picked up a wrench. "Maybe I should give her an adjustment before I depart tomorrow night!"

He set the wrench back down shaking his head. He had more important matters to attend to, and he doubted he had the courage to do such a thing. Moving from one tangle of wire and knobs to another, he made slight adjustments, calibrating knobs and switches on each. Wires ran along the floor here and there around the room. Finally he walked to one control panel that had dials and numbers on it like a combination lock.

"Damn," he said, eyebrows furrowing. The corners of his mouth dipped in a deep frown. "That hag has been messing with my machine, too. No matter, I will soon be rid of her once and for all."

There was a loud banging on the laboratory door.

"HENRY! Henry, I know you're in there. I know you can hear me. HENRY? What was that terrible racket you were making? I'm warning you, Henry...you pipe down in there or so help me I shall have everything you own thrown out into the street. Do you hear me, Henry? HENRY?"

Cowering behind his machine he waited, peeking over the top of the control panel until he heard her footsteps recede down the long hallway outside the door.

HAG! Mind your own business. Small-minded whelp of a woman. Making a racket? I haven't been making a racket. Pacing the floor, stepping carefully over wires, he put one hand over his mouth and puzzled. *Perhaps she's finally beginning to lose her mind.* He stopped, dropping his hands to his sides. *No. It would be years before I could have her declared insane.*

After changing the numbers on the dial back to their original setting, he tiptoed over to a control board and flipped a switch. A slight humming started to resonate from the capacitors and motors positioned around the room. Electrical currents buzzed through the wires.

He smiled.

Reaching toward a silver handle, he turned it. The machines clicked off and everything went silent.

What in the world? Henry checked the breaker boxes. None of the switches had tripped. The thought of turning the main breaker off and on crossed his mind, but then all the lights in the house would go off. That would definitely set the hag hammering on his door again.

Slamming his fist against the largest box in frustration, he tried to collect his thoughts. Without power it was just a useless hunk of metal. Something was definitely wrong, but he couldn't tell what.

"I can figure this out," he said walking around the room, carefully inspecting each control board until finally making his way back to the main. Opening the main access panel he immediately found the problem—the capacitor he had designed had burned itself out somehow. True, he had designed the capacitor to burn itself out, but only after a successful transfer. How the capacitor had managed to burn out on its own was puzzling and slightly troubling.

Well this is just great. It would take him at least a week to make another one from scratch. *I better get started.*

Frank Marshall was standing in front of the antique mirror his wife had decided to place on the wall in their living room.

What was I doing in here, he wondered. He looked down and realized he was holding the fire poker from the fireplace. There was something...something at the edge of his mind that he couldn't quite grab ahold of because his head was pounding terribly. He was going to do something with the fire poker...but what was it? Was he going to smash the mirror? It was possibly the largest mirror he had ever seen in his life—at least five feet wide and maybe four feet tall. An intricately hand- carved wood frame, flecked with gold, bordered the monstrosity. He couldn't imagine what in the world could have possessed her to buy such an ugly thing. He had been angry about the purchase for sure. But did his anger warrant him destroying the piece? No. Then why the fire poker?

He replaced it in its stand and checked his watch. He was late for work. He picked up his car keys preparing to leave, but just as his hand touched the doorknob, the phone began to ring stopping him in his tracks. He walked over and picked up the receiver.

"Hello?"

"Mr. Marshall?" The voice on the other end of the line belonged to Robert Westerly, the bellman at his apartment building.

"Yes, Robert. What can I do for you?"

"I'm sorry to bother you, Mr. Marshall, but Mrs. Watts from 509 called complaining about the noise from your apartment again."

"She must be mistaken, Robert, I wasn't making any noise. My wife is not in, so I'm pretty sure it wasn't her either. Is she sure she didn't just have her television set up too loud?"

"I'm not sure, but I'll tell them it must be someone else. Have a good day, Mr. Marshall."

"You do the same, Robert." Frank hung up the phone and stood for a moment. *What a strange woman, that Mrs. Watts.* This was the third time in as many weeks that she had called the apartment management about strange noises. Perhaps she's losing her mind. He hadn't heard any noises from anywhere. He certainly had not made any noise.

Frank walked back over to the mirror and straightened his tie. *That must have been what I came in here for earlier. Well, off to work.*

He grabbed his briefcase and walked out the door.

∴

Henry clicked the capacitor back into place and the circuit began to hum slightly.

"Ah, there we are. Good as new. Now let's get you all put back together." He screwed the panel back in place and turned on the viewing screen. His image faded from the reflective screen and was replaced by the image of a living room.

Empty...Oh well, I will just wait for her to get home. He had found the woman by pure accident. After the breakthrough of being able to transform simple mirrors into transmittable screens, he prepared several mirrors and donated them to thrift shops and antique stores around town. Most were purchased by people unsuitable for his needs. That was until recently, when an attractive woman was admiring herself in the mirror at a local antique store and trying to convince her husband to buy it.

Secretly, Frank had watched the entire exchange between the couple through the mirror. He had seen the man roll his eyes at her. He could tell the man didn't appreciate his wife the way that Henry would.

You don't know how lucky you are. You have such a beautiful wife—one that doesn't nag constantly.

He had watched them again, during their ride home. The woman kept glancing at the mirror in the car, and he imagined that she was looking at him.

Henry watched the man for several weeks and knew that he was unhappy. He felt that it wouldn't take much to convince the man to make the switch. However, it would require some deception.

Through the mirror he heard the sound of a door open. He heard the familiar clicking of the woman's high heels on the oak floor. She came into the living room and primped herself in front of the mirror.

"A new haircut, my dear?" Henry asked longingly. "And new polish on your nails to match your beautiful eyes."

"Ugh," she said suddenly. "Hand prints on my mirror again."

He heard the sound of the door again—heard the softer footsteps of the woman's husband, Frank. He watched as Frank walked meekly into the living room and sat down in a plush leather chair and picked up a magazine. The woman stared at Frank through the mirror's reflection. She put her arms on the fireplace mantel. She cocked her hips slightly, alluringly. Frank turned the page of his magazine, taking no notice of her.

Henry glared enviously at Frank.

"What a fool you are," he said from the other side of the mirror. "You do not see what a treasure you have. You don't deserve her. Tomorrow she will have a new husband. One that appreciates her."

He went back to preparing the machinery.

The next morning, Henry found Frank standing in front of the mirror straightening his tie. Henry watched him—loathed him. Stepping back from the mirror, Frank admired himself. A sharp electric sizzle made Frank duck his head. Then, he cocked his head to the side as if listening for something. He looked around his living room.

"Hello? Is someone there?" he shouted.

He turned back to the mirror and stumbled backwards at the shock of seeing not his own reflection, but another man, staring back at him. He yelled, backing away quickly—too quickly as it caused him to trip over his leather chair.

"Are you alright?" Henry asked.

Frank peeked over the chair at the mirror. He was sweating profusely, as if someone doused him with water. "Who are you? What do you want?"

"Sorry I frightened you," Henry said, not feeling sorry in the slightest. "My name is Henry Wingright. I'm an inventor and I've fabricated a machine that allows me to communicate to anyone through any mirror in the world." Henry smiled. This was a lie, of course. He could only communicate through mirrors he had prepared with the transmitter device. Frank didn't need to know this, however. The more the situation seemed like magic and less of a simple working of science, the better.

Frank stood up. He walked slowly to the mirror. "Why did you choose my mirror? What do you want?"

Henry shook his head. "You are direct, Frank, but I expected no less. What I have in mind could possibly benefit us both. I have been watching you for several days and—"

"Watching me?" Frank shouted. His hands balled into fists. "What do you mean you have been watching me?"

Henry held up his hands. "I apologize profusely, I didn't mean to spy but I needed to find the right person before I tried this. You see, I invented this device for more than one purpose, however the most pressing is...I want to escape from my life."

Frank relaxed his hands. Henry smiled. He could see that Frank was taking the bait.

"What do you mean escape from your life?" Frank asked.

Now to set the hook. "Well, you see, I'm not satisfied. I have a beautiful wife, a home, much the same as you. But I'm not happy. Have you ever been tired of the same old thing? The same daily grind?"

Frank nodded. He had.

"I thought so," Henry said. "The mirror is not only designed to communicate with another person, but also to trade places with that person."

Frank raised his eyebrows. "Trade places?"

"I have discovered a way to transfer the electrical impulses and energy, memories, personality... everything that makes a person who they are...from one person's brain into another and vice versa. To put it into less complicated terms—I would become you and you would become me." Henry smiled, waiting for frank to collect his thoughts.

"So," Frank began. "We would trade bodies...and no one would know?"

"Basically, that's true. It wouldn't be permanent, of course. We can always switch back. I have left instructions over here on how that can be done if you change your mind." Another lie. Henry had no intentions of ever coming back to this life. The load capacitor would burn itself out after the transfer and he was the only one who knew how to design another one.

"So, what do you say? Care to give it a try?"

Frank rubbed his chin. "Will it hurt?" he asked.

"I'm not sure," Henry said, thinking this truth wouldn't hurt his chances. "I've never actually made a transfer before, but I wouldn't think so."

Frank thought for a moment. He did want to be rid of this mundane existence. Everything—his wife, family, home, career—was covered in a shroud of apathy. Life had lost its luster long ago. This was a chance for change. A once-in-a-lifetime opportunity. He didn't think that once Henry transferred into his body he would think this life was any better. Maybe Henry would want to switch back. Frank smiled. That wouldn't be a problem. If he switched, he would be the one in control of the machine. Even if Henry begged, Frank wouldn't have to change back.

"Alright," Frank said. "How do we do this?"

I've got you. Henry resisted the urge to clap and cheer. "All you need to do is place your hands on the mirror and I will place my hands on the screen on this side."

Frank put his hands on the mirror. Henry flipped some switches and a loud humming and electrical droning began. The sound reverberated throughout Frank's living room. He wanted to cover his ears but didn't want to take his hands away from the mirror. Henry walked over and placed his hands on the view screen.

Frank laughed to himself. *She'll be mad when she comes home and finds handprints on her mirror again.* Moments later, he was staring at a blank screen in a dirty basement—the noise from the machine gone.

Frank looked around at the decrepit surroundings. He saw papers stacked on tables. Assorted tools were lying on workbenches around the room. He walked over to a large table in the center of the room littered with drawings and diagrams, searching for the instructions on how the machine worked. He found nothing.

"They're not here," Frank said, his voice rising in pitch. "Where are they? Where are the instructions?" He threw useless papers onto the floor.

Henry was watching Frank through the mirror. He saw his body moving around, but knew it wasn't him anymore. He had a new body now. He stepped back from the mirror as the power in the machine leeched out, and the image faded. He flexed his muscles, which were much harder than the ones he had just left behind. He sauntered over and grabbed the fire poker. He would break the mirror and be rid of his old life once and for all.

Suddenly, there was a searing pain in his head. He felt as though someone was digging through his brain with a hot needle. He felt all of his memories tumbling away, being replaced by people and things he didn't remember. He started to scream.

Frank was still rifling through papers scattered about the room, when the same pain that plagued Henry hit him. He felt like someone was flaying his brain with a potato peeler. His memories began to tumble away, replaced by the memories of someone else.

He screamed.

The men on either side of the portal sounded their pain in a harmony of torment. They fell to the floor simultaneously.

Frank stood in front of the mirror. He was trying to remember what he had come in here for. Why was he holding the fire poker? Something *about the mirror*. He walked over and put the poker back where it belonged.

I was going to do something with the mirror. His head was pounding. It was too hard to think straight.

Henry stood in his laboratory.

Now what was he doing again? Oh, yes. That's right. I was making the final adjustments on the machine. He made a mental note to clean up his work area. Tools were knocked over and papers scattered on the table. He didn't remember making such a mess. His head was pounding terribly.

Everest

ॐ

S. Rey

The sunlight reflecting off the sand blinds him temporarily as he shuffles his feet, repeating to himself, "Right, left, right, left." He does all he can to will his tired body forward. The hot, dry sand attempts to anchor him in place. He glances in the distance where the lake awaits. It's there, he sees it, but whether he will make it or not he is unsure.

He's been in this deserted place for what feels like days, although he can't remember why, or how he got there. He only knows if he doesn't get to the water soon, he will die. Sweat beads down his brow dripping into his eye. He stops to rub it out and immediately regrets his decision. It's almost impossible to get moving after even the briefest of pauses.

Maybe he should rest anyway. He cannot remember how long he's been walking.

He pulls off his pack and sets it in the sand. He sits with a groan as the mere act assaults the pain receptors throughout his body. The lake sits in the distance, unwavering. Taunting him with its sparkling reflection. The heat is becoming unbearable—his tongue is dry, throat parched. How much longer can he go without water?

He removes his shirt and crumples it up into a makeshift pillow. The sand burns his bare back as he lays his head down, but that does not bother him. He knows he must rest—cannot fight the urge any longer.

The sun is almost directly overhead now. Was it even in the sky when he started his trek? He doesn't know.

He is just beginning to doze when a sound annoyingly pulls him from his peace.

"Flynn..." A male voice calls his name in the distance.

He struggles to sit up. Something about the voice is menacing. It makes him uncomfortable. He searches in every direction but cannot find the source.

"Hey, Flynn!"

His head jerks around. There in the distance behind him he sees a shape approaching. Is he imagining things? Is someone really calling him? A glimmer of hope clears his muddled thoughts momentarily. Maybe they can explain how the hell he got into the middle of the desert!

He squints into the form, which is steadily growing larger as it moves toward him.

"Who *are* you?" Flynn asks, still unable to make out distinct features.

The figure does not respond but continues moving—quickly now. Flynn's heart begins to speed up, adrenaline taking the place of exhaustion.

Something is not right.

The sun reflects off something in the figure's hand, temporarily blinding Flynn, distracting his thoughts. He moves to the side, avoiding the bright beam. The man's hand hangs loosely at his side, but it's clear he is gripping the object tightly. Whatever it is, this man does not want to drop it. Flynn stands, focusing on the approaching person and the mysterious object. He sees now that the man is wearing a long jacket—what appears to be a winter jacket. It covers dark pants and large spiked boots. Who would dress like this in the middle of the desert? Suddenly, the man makes a move with the strange object. He bends his elbow and brings it up. The light reflects long enough for Flynn to realize what it is.

A knife.

The man is wielding a knife and coming quickly.

"Hey now, I don't want any trouble!" Flynn pleads, preparing to run.

The man does not stop.

Will not stop.

He is a mere twenty feet away now when Flynn notices something that turns his blood cold. Where there should have been a face, there is nothing but an empty black void.

"What the fuck?!" Flynn exclaims.

After only a moment's hesitation he turns to run.

"Flynn!" The man calls after him.

Flynn does not stop, does not turn to look. He runs as fast as he can, leaving his belongings behind. He runs for his life, terror pushing him faster than he can comprehend.

But the man is on his heels now, and Flynn realizes there will be no escape. This man is too fast and he is just too tired. All the nightmare-inspired adrenaline in the world cannot make up for the dehydration and sheer exhaustion wrecking his body and mind.

He halts abruptly hoping to surprise his attacker and swings his fist. His aim was true and he hit the man squarely on the forearm, sending the blade flying into the sand. The man is surprised just long enough for Flynn to be the first to reach the knife. He snatches it up and turns toward the faceless figure.

The man advances, unwavering, shoulders hunched in an aggressive stance.

"Flynn...it's okay..."

Flynn knows better. He is exhausted, dehydrated, disoriented, but he knows something is wrong with this man. And at this point it is his life or the stranger's. It is a choice that is made without a second thought as Flynn pounces, burying the blade into the man's chest. He pulls it out quickly and stabs again.

The man sinks to the ground, arms instinctively covering his wounds.

He still has no face.

Flynn does not feel remorse. He knows he would have died on this day had he not turned the tables.

He leaves the man behind, gurgling—attempting to speak. Flynn does not care what he has to say. Flynn moves on, his pace quickened, determined now to reach the lake.

It is not long before his exhaustion catches up with him, however. The lake does not seem to be getting any closer either. He begins to wonder if he should just rest a moment, but knows if he does that, he will not get up again.

He has only made it another few hundred feet when movement catches his eye. He turns to see two more men approaching from the left. However, these two are not only in thick heavy clothes, but they have some sort of masks covering their faces.

"God dammit!" What was happening? Flynn silently searches his memories, attempting to grasp any floating thread he can. There is nothing there. He has no idea who these men are or why they're attacking him in the desert.

"Hey Flynn!" One of the men calls to him.

Flynn stops, curious if they will attack like the last one. It doesn't take long before he sees the same disturbing signs he saw with the last man. They wore masks covering their mouth and nose, however there were no eyes. Devoid of any color, they were a black pit.

Flynn's stomach tightens with fear. He looks them up and down, in search of a weapon. There is none that he sees, but judging by stature and stance, he knows he will be unable to outrun them. He turns to face his attackers and readies the bloody knife still clutched in his hand.

The first one to reach him makes a move toward the knife, but Flynn is fast—fight or flight adrenaline courses his veins and pumps his heart. He slaps the man's hand away and thrusts the blade into his exposed throat—straight into the jugular vein. Flynn removes the knife, stepping back to watch the man fall. He will be dead in moments.

He looks up to see the other one hesitating. They square off. Who will attack first? Neither of them knows. Flynn considers waiting, running—anything but taking yet one more life. He quickly realizes the element of surprise may just be the only thing currently on his side. He leaps toward the man, wrapping his arms around him, burying the still-sharp blade in his back—just to the left of the spine.

He jumps back, unable to pull the weapon out, and instead turns to run. He doubts the man will follow, but flees regardless. He cannot keep doing this. He is not a killing machine. Is he? He doesn't know anymore. He runs for what seems like hours but never seems to get any closer to the water. He feels as though he is moving uphill. His bones and muscles scream at him with every movement forward.

They beg him to stop.

To please rest.

Eventually he can take no more and concedes to the imploring of his body. He falls to the sandy floor, no longer able to even muster the strength to hold himself up. He can only lay still, trying to calm his screaming muscles.

Night has fallen. Stars speckle the sky providing a soft soothing glow. The beauty of the dark urges thoughts and images into Flynn's mind. Memories begin to flash before his eyes. He sees his two children, a boy and a girl. Flynn remembers the family he's left behind.

His wife.

Kristin.

At the thought of her name his heart is torn in two.

His beloved.

He recalls kissing her and the children goodbye. Their faces smiling up at him as he assures them he'll be back soon. Will they be okay without him?

The nagging questions return...why did he leave? How did he end up here? Where the hell is 'here'?

"My love..." His voice is weak. So weak. He can't fight anymore.

"I love you," he says. His eyes slowly close as he loses his battle for survival. A single tear drops into the sand and he expels his last breath into the darkness that awaits him.

"I think they are somewhere just below Camp 4..." Thomas calls down to his friend who is harnessed below him on the mountain. He continues climbing, relentless. Knowing that every moment wasted could be their friend's last.

James responds by climbing faster as well, digging his spiked boots in deep with each step.

The sun shining brightly in the sky does little to dissuade the cold snaking its way throughout his body. They continue their climb in silence. Lhotse Wall is no place to fuck around. It is not until Camp 4 is within view that the silence is broken.

"Shit," Thomas stops dead in his tracks nearly knocking James off the mountain. He opens his mouth in protest, but is immediately hushed when his eyes catch what Thomas' already have. Last night's blizzard had left mounds of snow piled sporadically about and they were partially blanketed in white, but they were there—unmistakable articles of clothing poking out as if clawing for the day's warmth and unimpeded air.

James' blood runs cold—completely unrelated to the sub-zero temperature—as the realization hits him; they may already be too late.

After further examination they find two bodies there in the snow, huddled close together making James think they died around the same time. He struggles to hold back the vomit making its way up its throat as he stares at the deep gash in his friend's neck. It takes only a moment to notice they are also surrounded by blood. Had there not been a blizzard last night, there would be rumors below of a bleeding mountain.

Jack was not another hapless victim of the beast that is Everest.

After brushing some snow aside, the appearance of a knife makes it clear Steve also died violently.

"What the hell?" Thomas asks aloud. "Who could have done this?"

James merely shakes his head, unable to think.

"There's another one," Thomas notes, abruptly cutting through the profound silence that now blankets the mountain.

They apprehensively make their way toward the third body—now only barely covered in snow.

There is blood all over the front of his body, and his arms lay frozen in an attempt to protect his vital organs.

"What the fuck happened?!" James could feel anger rising now. Who would have killed his friends and...

James and Thomas exchange glances, sharing their next thought.

"Where's..."

"Flynn?" Thomas finishes James question.

It only takes a moment of searching before they see him. A distance away—his mask, boots, jacket and shirt have been removed. He lays in the snow, frozen, partially dressed, eyes closed. His right hand is covered in small gashes and blood. He clearly had been the one wielding the weapon.

The friends know immediately what had happened. They recall the frantic conversations via walkie-talkie that took place the night before. Flynn's mental state had been deteriorating rapidly. Steve, Derek and Jack had tried to get him down before the storm hit, but they didn't make it.

Thomas and James were unable to come to their aid until now.

Apparently, now was too late.

They both knew altitude sickness all too well. They knew what it is capable of doing to the mind. They had heard the stories of delirium and hallucinations. They knew that when hypothermia is added to the mix, it can become a deadly combination. And not just for the victim.

James sighs as he picks up Flynn's jacket several yards from his body. He covers him with it and then stands in mournful silence trying to comprehend what has happened.

It is not long before he is nudged by Thomas. The hardest part—the climb down—is yet to come and they cannot afford to waste any more time or oxygen, lest they join their friends in snowy graves.

They begin making their way down leaving their friends behind. Their bodies frozen in time along with the many other souls Mt. Everest has claimed.

Evil Seed

Bruce H. Markuson

My name is Dr. David Riley. This is my story. I am writing more for myself than any future generation. The main reason I am writing is for one question: when I die, in my day of judgment, when I have to face my maker, I wonder...how will I be judged? How will I be judged for what I have done?

Much of my story comes from my own recollection and the records from my court case. I did not witness the micro-apocalypse that killed half a billion people, even though I caused it. Instead, I kept myself isolated. I remember guiding my electric wheelchair from the biohazard truck through a clear plastic tube into the courtroom.

The tube led to my bio chamber. It was a

hermetically sealed glass box situated in the middle of the crowded old-fashioned courtroom decorated with elaborate polished-wood cornice molding.

Dozens of cameras were pointed at me. People were shouting, "Why did you do it? Dr. Riley, are you the one who released the virus?"

Judge Walker pounded his gavel. "Quiet please, I will be asking all the questions for Dr. Riley."

The courtroom immediately became silent. Then Judge Walker and the prosecutor continued with all the official court proceedings and statements. He went through all the legal details that I confess I did not pay much attention to.

I have looked at a video of myself sitting in that courtroom. My oxygen tank is connected to my nose, and I have that tube in my lungs that is constantly making a sucking noise. My left hand is curled up against my side. I can use it for little more than typing on my computer. My right eye is missing, replaced with a glass one. I was a brilliant but timid man. My face was sagging. I was not used to talking much.

I don't look like the monster everyone has made me out to be, unless you label me 'that mad scientist.'

In the past few years I'd spent most of my life alone. I had set up a cot in the bio chamber in my laboratory. Only recently did the police find me. Ironically, they were seeking me only because they knew I was an expert on viral studies. After the virus was released, the authorities sought many experts in the field. My name was on that list. When all attempts to contact me had failed, they sent the police to break into my laboratory.

Inside they found many files and glass Petri dishes marked "Evil Seed." Soon, it was discovered that I had a stockpile of the virus. And after my hard drive was examined they quickly realized they had found their culprit. I was not working for some rogue nation. I was not a terrorist or a member of a cult. This was purely my own independent work.

The huge media coverage took all of my attention. Judge Walker, an older man with a receded hairline, was looking down his nose over his reading classes at me. I vaguely recall him asking, "Dr. Riley, how do you plead?"

I did not answer.

"Dr. Riley," Judge Walker raised his voice. "You have been charged with producing and releasing an air-born virus. The release of the virus has killed over four hundred and forty million people. How do you plead?"

The bailiff in the courtroom was an elderly man of about seventy. He knocked on the glass of my bio chamber.

"The judge asked you a question," he pressed.

I looked up at Judge Walker and simply said, "Your Honor."

The judge started to get upset, then quickly composed himself. I was pleased to see that I was becoming quite good at observing peoples' responses after the virus was released. It seems that human beings have changed significantly. The judge looked as if he might raise his voice, but did not. The anger did not arise within him.

"Dr. Riley, you have chosen to represent yourself in this case," Judge Walker repeated in a calm, cool, methodical voice. "You have been charged with releasing The Virus. You have been charged with the murder of one out of seventeen people on the entire planet Earth—almost half a billion people. I will need to know how you plead."

"Did I do something wrong?" I asked.

Judge Walker took a deep breath, then slowly let it out. I observed that the anger tried to build up in him, but quickly subsided. The higher-order functions of his brain remained in control. He stayed calm even though it appeared like he wanted to get upset.

He looked at the clerk and said, "Margret, may I see Dr. Riley's psychological evaluation again? And please call up Bill at the public defender's office. He has a client."

"No, Your Honor," I remarked. "It is my right to defend myself. I...I plead guilty."

A loud murmuring went through the courtroom.

Judge Walker picked up his gavel, ready to strike. He leaned into the microphone.

"Could everyone please quiet down?" he said.

The courtroom was immediately silenced. Judge Walker looked at his gavel and gently put it down.

The gavel was not needed. Though people were shocked by the verdict, it seemed that everyone realized they were in a court of law.

My observations were confirmed. Emotions did not rule the higher-order functions of the brain. Human beings are changing.

"Dr. Riley, I want you to explain to this court why you did this," Judge Walker demanded. "Why? You are a very wealthy man as a result of the patents you have developed in the field of virology. You have eliminated many other viral diseases from the world. You are considered the foremost authority in many aspects of your field. You have not gained anything by doing this. Why? Why did you do this?"

Still, he was not getting upset. He was simply asking me a question, looking for the answers.

So I said to Judge Walker, "I thought it was a good thing to do. Perhaps it got out of hand."

"Out of hand?" He paused for a moment, then calmly said, "Dr. Riley, I want you to explain to this court what you mean by 'out of hand.' Are you saying that half a billion people are worthy of being killed, because you believe they are psychotic killers?"

"No, Your Honor. I am saying that half a billion people have the capability to do incredible harm in this world. I had thought the worst of the worst would only be affected. I could not have foreseen that so many people could be so evil or have the potential to be so evil.

"If someone is not evil by nature," I continue, slowly. "If someone has a few skeletons in their closet but would not commit horrible acts—if that person has capability to empathize with other people, then that person's mind will very simply have to rethink and function differently." I leaned forward, as best I could in my wheelchair. "But there were many, I knew, who would be walking down the street and suddenly drop. Their brains could no longer function after being infected with the virus."

I settled back, my sagging face trying to give a positive look. "If evil is the core of a person's being, then yes, they will die. But that is okay, I calculated, and probably for the best. These were mostly criminals. Members of criminal organizations, gangs and gang members, drug dealers, members of drug cartels. Dictators, members of armies of dictatorships. Those who don't care about the suffering of others, but take pleasure in profiting by exploiting the misfortunes of their poor victims."

I looked the judge straight in the eye. "Jesus once said: *'Where there is a corpse, there the vultures gather.'*"

After a brief pause I continued. "Before the virus was released, one percent of the U.S. population was in prison and twice that number probably should have been. Another three percent would do or have done the same such terrible things if, and when, given the opportunity...or if they did not fear the authorities. The world is full of good people, but one in seventeen, I have calculated, have sold their souls to the devil."

The judge sat back and pondered that statement.

"Dr. Riley, years ago I may have dismissed that statement as just another ramblings of a defendant. That was before the virus. But now after evaluating it from my own experience sitting at this court, I would have to agree with your assessment."

He looked oddly calm about his statement, as if his rational brain was convinced.

"Dr. Riley, how did this all start?" he asked.

"It all started when I was twelve years old," I began. "I lived in a nice little suburb. Then two boys from the neighborhood, Fred and Todd, were walking down the sidewalk carrying their daddy's .22 rifle. They saw me and thought it would be funny to shoot. The first bullet hit my spine and I fell to the sidewalk. They got a good laugh out of that. The second shot went through my arm and lodged in my lung. The third went through my eye and out the side of my head. They stepped on me as they walked off leaving me for dead. An elderly lady in the neighborhood heard the gun shots and—"

"Fred and Todd Danner?" The Judge interrupted. "Those two were serial killers. Were you their first victim?"

"No, Your Honor. I was their second or third victim. Their first victim was a seven-year-old girl. I don't want to tell you what they did to her. People did not find out about her until years later. I was their first known victim, and the first one to identify the two of them. Since I was not killed, they were sent to juvenile prison and released before they became adults. After they were let out, they ran away from home and went on their killing spree. Those two were just evil." My voice was quiet, under complete control. "It was at that time I wanted to understand *why*. So, I decided to dedicate my life to finding out why. I became a doctor of pathology, neurology, and forensic psychology. I wanted to see inside the human mind. Eventually, I added my doctorate in virology.

"I have studied the human mind for many years. I have dissected numerous brains by MRI, slicing and digitizing them into 3D images, and also by physically dissecting the human brain tissue. Under electron microscopes, I have looked at every aspect of both human and primate brains.

"I began my studies with chimpanzees. When a leopard comes too near a group of chimpanzees, the males will take six-foot long sticks and beat it to death. That is higher-order thinking. It is helpful to their survival. However, chimpanzees will go to war with each other—also higher-order thinking, but detrimental to their survival.

"I have seen all-too-human behavior in chimpanzees. For example, a group of male chimpanzees were chasing a young baboon. The males were extremely hyped up for the hunt. Their adrenalin was high, and the pleasure center of their brains was on overdrive. The young baboon got away—their need was not satisfied. They came back to their band and killed one of there own baby chimpanzees from their band despite the screams of its mother. They tore it apart and ate it to satisfy their need for the kill. They could do nothing wrong."

"Dr. Riley, these are animals with natural predatory instincts," Judge Walker challenged.

"No, Your Honor. Chimpanzees are not predators by nature. They are basically vegetarians. They have over 99% the same DNA as humans. Still, you may think of them as cute little monkeys, but they can be vicious animals. That is the higher-order behavior of their minds being influenced by their animal instinct. So, I found myself thinking, 'What if I could disconnect that?'"

"Dr. Riley, I resent when you compare people to chimpanzees," Judge Walker replied. "One thing that I have seen all too often in the criminal mind is that when someone is dehumanized, it is easier to harm or kill that person than when they are thought of as your equal."

"You are absolutely right, Your Honor. I have also studied the brains of career criminals—I studied them all. Terrorists, mobsters, serial killers, slumlords, con men who rob people of their life savings. I examined the brain of a man who owned a chemical company. He dumped fifty barrels of toxic waste into the river and killed over three hundred people. He didn't care. I have found a positive correlation to those chimpanzees' brains."

"Dr. Riley, there is far more profound philosophy of what is right and wrong other than just not caring, Judge Walker added. "Humans are capable of deciding what is right and wrong."

I cleared my throat. "One of the major characteristics of psychotic behavior is the inability to empathize with others."

Judge Walker nodded. "I see your point, Dr. Riley."

"Do we, as humans, let the higher-order functions of our brains control our animal instincts?" I asked. "Or do we let our animal instincts control the higher-order functions of our brain? Are *right* and *wrong* merely words with no deeper meaning? You are absolutely right, Your Honor, people can decide right and wrong and do choose wrong.

"The Roman historian Tacitus knew this two thousand years ago when he wrote of the Roman soldier: *'Opinions varied widely on what was right. Nobody believed that they could do anything wrong.'*

"What is right is then replaced with what is right for the Fatherland, the Motherland, the Homeland, the Company, the Brotherhood, the Cartel; your people, our side, the leader, the family, the Fuhrer. If someone makes excuses for the atrocities they commit, and those excuses are accepted, then their brain is becoming rewired.

"And soon, anyone who is not part of it is what

you have said yourself, Your Honor: They would be considered 'subhuman.' Fred and Todd thought of me as subhuman and took pleasure in using me as target practice. I did the autopsy on the brain of Fred Danner. He was stabbed in a prison fight. He was evil to the core."

"Define evil to the core," Judge Walker asked.

"Evil to the core is when someone has completely abandoned any sense of empathy for their fellow human being. And some even take pleasure in harming others. I could see inside the brain that had done me such harm. The brain pattern correlated."

"Correlated?"

"Yes, Your Honor. I discovered a correlation of evil. In my research, I found the account of a woman who survived the Nazi concentration camps who once said of the guards: *'These were not devils with horns; These were just boys.'* I was able to procure the preserved brain of a guard from a Nazi concentration camp. That was my final research. I was able to generalize the specific points in the brain where the need to shout 'Heil Hitler' had overridden the point in the brain that shouts, 'It is wrong to push these people into the gas chamber!'

"For someone so heavily indoctrinated, their sense of right and wrong was lost. They were told what was right and what was wrong. And to question what they were told was wrong to question. That was the last research I needed. I had found it."

"Found what?" asked the judge.

"The Evil Seed," I said.

"Could you better explain that?"

"I observed the neurobiology of evil. How evil is manifested in the brain. There are differences in neurological activity and blood flow to the brain in the evil mind. There are three specific areas of the brain that are affected. It all starts in the Amygdala located in the primitive limbic system in the brain. If not functioning properly a person would not care or not have concern for another human being.

"Then there is a connection to the Orbital Frontal Cortex. That is the more frontal portion of the brain. A higher order function, which has the capability of deciding right from wrong. Your moral fortitude. This part might put the brakes on. But if the signal is weak or bypassed from the Amygdala to the Orbital Frontal Cortex—if either is not functioning properly or if that person has been heavily indoctrinated—right and wrong become words with no deeper meaning.

"Finally, it relates to how it interacts with the Anterior Cingulate Cortex. This is a higher order function centrally located in the brain. Sort of a mind of its own—your inner conscience. For example, if a soldier goes to war and does not care about the enemy or may even find it right to kill the enemy...when ordered to wholesale slaughter civilians—this 'inner conscience' is the jury. The part of the brain that would say 'bad move' and might reason that we are better than that. It allows us to think about the ramifications of our actions. This is the part of the brain that most heavily affected by indoctrination. If, in the end, this part is being damaged, altered or rewired—that is the Evil Seed.

"Your Honor, I very intensively engineered the virus to only attack the brains of people who were evil. This virus can therefore rewrite the DNA code of the human species. A person would have to be one of three things to have died from the virus: Heavily indoctrinated, culturally adapted and a complete sellout to a lawless society or just evil by nature. Most people's minds simply are not affected or would slightly rewire and live on.

"I sent Todd Danner a package of candy and marked it, 'From your biggest fan.' He was the first recipient of the virus. The guards at the prison said he was dead before he hit the floor. Evil was the core of his being."

"I see," Judge Walker simply stated, then added, "Dr. Riley, I am a deer hunter and I admit I get a rush out of stalking and hunting down a buck. I enjoy the killing when I fire that single shot. Now, I still hunt—to keep down the deer population and put some meat on my table, but it is no longer the same. If you look around the courtroom, Dr. Riley..." Judge Walker gestured to the room. "There are no lynch mobs. No angry protesters. No one is out for blood. We have become a world calmly watching the news reports, calmly seeking justice. Because of you, people want answers and justice to be served. Not just revenge.

"Dr. Riley, three wars were going on in the world. A few leaders were strongly considering the nuclear option because of atrocities committed. That all stopped after the release of the virus.

"I want you to listen to me very carefully, Doctor. You may have, just possibly, avoided World War Three. I have been put in a great dilemma." Judge Walker held up a hand full of documents. "A half-dozen nations have given you diplomatic immunity and have offered you refuge. Yet, given the extreme magnitude of your crime, offering you refuge would create enormous conflicts with certain other nations. I have been put in quite a predicament—one that I have never had to deal with in thirty years of sitting at this bench in this courtroom.

"I have conversed with the world court and many of the world's leaders...I offered a compromise. Through much debate and extensive arguing back and forth, all have come together and agreed on the best way that justice can be served. First of all, you are a citizen and resident of this jurisdiction. You will be judged in this court and this court only. Otherwise you would be spending the rest of your natural life going from trial to trial.

"Furthermore, I would like to better understand your motives. Dr. Riley, is all this because you could not take revenge on those two boys, so you took it out on the rest of the world?"

That was not said out of malice. That was the voice of experience.

I reflected for a moment. "I always thought that I was doing the right thing."

"Dr. Riley, how do I pass sentence on a crime of this magnitude while others call you a hero? Some even wish to award you with the Nobel peace prize. This may seem unorthodox, but your sentence was discussed with the world court prior to your pleading guilty." Judge Walker gestured to the bailiff and said, "Bailiff, if you please."

I panicked. "No, Your Honor. Perhaps I could do community service by doing research for charitable organizations."

"I am sure that you will be doing that anyway, Dr. Riley. I fully empathize with you, but this is the best way." The judge gestured to the bailiff once again. "Bailiff, if you please."

I screamed out, "Please, Your Honor, I pleaded guilty! I did commit this crime! I should stay in prison. I beg of you...perhaps we could work out another type of arrangement. I only decided—"

"Who are you to decide the fate of half a billion people?" Judge Walker interrupted. "Who made you the judge of all humanity? You think you can judge all of humanity by sitting in your lab dissecting brains?"

"Your Honor, please," I pleaded. "I implore you. I did not mean to do anything wrong."

Judge Walker looked at me. "We shall soon see. Dr. Riley, you are free to go."

The bailiff walked up to the door of my bio chamber. He quickly figured out how it unlatched and opened the door. A burst of air rushed out. The bailiff walked in and pushed my wheelchair out into the courtroom and faced me to the judge. Dozens of cameras in the courtroom were pointed at me. People stood there like a flock of vultures waiting to see if I would drop dead. Yet, as I observed, they meant me no harm. Now I would face my own creation.

Judge Walker made his pronouncement. "Dr. Riley, your license to practice medicine has been revoked. All your equipment has been confiscated. You will not be allowed to work in the field of virology. You are truly an embarrassment to the medical profession. I hope that you will find more worthy pursuits in your career."

I was angry. He exposed me to the virus, revoked my license, took my equipment. How dare he? How dare he insult my professionalism? How dare he question my intentions? I have accomplished more things alone in my lab than whole institutes, in fact, more than whole countries even dreamed about. I felt an adrenalin rush. I was about to lash out at him.

But then I took a few breaths of air. And a moment later, I felt the angry feeling slowly die away in me.

Instead, I said to Judge Walker, "I understand your reasoning. I can see that you have made the right decision. I may have made the same decision if I were in your place. It seems that the harshest judgment is that I will have to face up to my own hypocrisy, my own creation, to face the virus. Isn't this the very judgment that I have put upon the rest of humanity? It is poetic justice."

"I have sat on this bench in this criminal court for more than thirty years," Judge Walker responded. "I have seen the worst and lowest criminals walk in and out of this courtroom. And many it has been my privilege and pleasure to send to prison. But I can see that you are not a criminal. Of all the evil people in this world, you are not among them. And there are a lot of evil people in this world."

Then I answered, "Not anymore."

The Auxiliary Bishop of Hell

Gene Hines

*D*edicated to Marjorie Bowen.

The Reverend Doctor Robert King Ray was pastor of the largest church in Miami. The membership of the church had a mix of corporate executives and wealthy real estate brokers. On Sunday mornings the parking lot looked like a Lexus dealership.

Robert King Ray was also chairman of the committees of half a dozen charitable organizations, a member of the most fashionable country club in Miami, where he played golf with senators, congressmen, and corporate execs, and he was a member of Mensa. He held a doctorate from Vanderbilt. He was smooth, smart, and imminently presentable—a golden boy. He could hold a smile longer than any man alive. And he was evil.

I first personally met Robert Ray when he shook my hand at the front doors of the church one Sunday after services. He invited me for a drink. Ministers of his congregation are permitted at least a sniff of alcohol on occasion. He thanked me for some legal work I had done for the church. There was a question about the boundaries of the church's property and I fixed it for them. Not a great legal accomplishment, but enough to get me introduced to the Rev. Dr. Ray.

I didn't travel in the circles of congressmen or real estate tycoons, and I couldn't afford the most exclusive country club in Miami. Neither was I a member of Mensa. So, it surprised me, free legal work or not, that the Reverend Doctor would offer to spend some time with me.

It was, I know now, because he saw the same thing in me that was in himself. How he saw it, I don't know. I had never seen it myself; it was latent, waiting for a catalyst like Robert Ray to set it going. I didn't know I loved the same things Robert Ray did until he showed me it was so.

I lived by the rules, got an education, paid my taxes, didn't cheat on my wife, and provided free legal services for the local school board and Robert Ray's church. I was in the Air National Guard. I was the ideal middle-class American; I lived well, if not extravagantly. I had all I needed, including Cheryl, my redheaded wife. I had a house in the upper-middle-class section of a suburb of Miami. I was a good conventional man and I had the material success to prove it in the conventional American way. All that is gone now.

First, there was that polite little drink in Robert Ray's study. Then we had lunch together. Then lunch again. Then with our wives; we had dinner out, and in our homes. Things progressed; we vacationed together as families a couple of times, to see the fall leaves in the Appalachians. One Christmas, we went to Jamaica together. All so normal, so conventional, so much the life of well educated, well-to-do people.

If I wondered at first why Robert Ray—golden-boy minister, member of Mensa, celebrity on the cover of *Gold Coast Magazine*—and I were friends, I squandered any doubts quickly enough. It was too much fun. It was what I thought the world owed me for being well educated intelligent, diligent, good-looking, and normal—it was the world as it should be. It was the American dream and gradually Robert seduced me into his secret life.

He taught me to play golf. He introduced me to a congressman or two. He stood for me to join the county club and loaned me the money for it. We played golf, had drinks, and ate dinner at the club with our wives, along with all the other socializing we did. I never questioned it, why should I? I was on the way up and would soon, I was sure, pass into the elite of the community, if not the whole city.

One night, instead of the club bar, we, Robert and I, went to Robert's *gentleman's club*. As I know now, all the things we did—the golf and the introductions, the vacation in Jamaica—all of it, was leading up to that point. We had been palling around for months now and it was time, I'm sure Robert thought, to reel me in.

"Well, how do you like it?" he asked.

"Like what?" I said, the ice rattling in my drink as I put it down on the bar.

"This." He smiled his golden smile and swept his hand around the room.

"I like it fine," I replied. "Didn't know what I was missing all these years." I smiled back, telling a little fib. I didn't actually think much of the place.

It was called the *Fox Club*. It was redneck, despite the parking lot full of cars that looked like the ones parked at Robert's church every Sunday morning. If anyone in that building knew who Robert was, and some must have, they gave no hint of recognition—they were all *gentlemen* with something to lose and so they kept their mouths shut. That was the rule of the place. It was slumming for the upper-middle-class.

The darkness inside was broken by lights on a stage, cigarette and cigar smoke, along with smoke of a decidedly weedy odor. Middle-aged and well-dressed men, band noise, and naked girls completed the atmosphere.

We spent two hours drinking top-shelf bourbon, smoking what Robert said were genuine Cuban cigars, and stuffing money into the hands of the naked girls; they didn't have any place else to put it. They took their money to a back room and came back for more.

Soon, drinking the top-shelf bourbon, the light in the place was a mellow bronze color and the inside of my head was churning out sweet haze-edged dreams.

Then Robert starting obsessing about one particular girl. She was stark naked, like all the other dancers and waitresses. She was a redhead.

"I just love that red-haired pussy," Robert said, over the clamor of the country band.

I'm a pretty sophisticated man but the sound of clergyman; one of the best known clergymen in Miami, saying such a thing left me speechless. Robert laughed, slapped me on the back and said, "Loosen up."

There was no stopping him after that. We went to the club often. Robert was a favorite customer. He had his own table, drinks were brought to him without the necessity of asking for them. He was treated like royalty. The girls took turns sidling up to his table and rubbing their naked bodies against him, grinding and cooing. Robert made it known that he needed two girls at his table from now on, and so I got my own grinding and cooing.

One night there was a scuffle in one corner; men dust devil fighting and shouting at one another. A black man, shouted, "She's mine! I paid! I paid!" with a French accent, as other men shoved him out of a back door. Robert laughed and said, "Not all of us are *gentlemen* it would seem."

Robert had an apartment in Cutler Bay and we took *Fox* girls there. He took the redhead most of the time. But the apartment only had one bedroom and so, at first, my girl-of-the-day and I, got the couch-pullout in the living room. Then we started sharing the bedroom. We traded girls. Sometimes I would catch Robert looking at me with open delight—he was glorying in my enticement into his secret life.

This secret life was managed with extraordinary skill. The *Fox Club* opened early, by three in the afternoon, so Robert, and now *we*, could get in and get it all done and be home by dinner. His wife knew nothing. And neither did mine. She paid no heed to any smell of booze; lawyers have a drink or two for lunch or after the office closes, don't they? Perfume? The girls weren't allowed to wear any, one of Robert's stipulations in doing business with the club. The smell of sex? A quick shower.

Once a week, to the club at three, take in a few nude dances, a grinding and cooing apiece, a drink or two, then off to the apartment with the redhead and the girl I fancied at the time, and then home by no later than eight. It worked. And I spent a lot of days *working late*, nothing unusual for an up-and-coming lawyer. I worked weekends sometimes, too. All so skillfully done. And, after six months we went to a new, even lower, level; to what Robert was planning all along.

One Sunday, after services, he invited me to his study.

"I've got something to talk to you about." He actually winked at me. "Sit down," he said, handing me a cigar.

Robert's study was lined with books—they almost circled the room. I smoked the cigar and watched the smoke weave itself above our heads, until Robert spoke again.

"I have a proposition to make," he stated.

We were sitting in leather chairs in front of his double-sized mahogany desk. I was eager to hear this proposition; I knew it would be the culmination of my apprenticeship into deception and pleasure. I took a long draw from the cigar.

"Actually, it's a wager," Robert said. "A bet."

My face must have showed my surprise.

"You weren't expecting that, I see." He laughed and took a puff from his own cigar then sat back to watch the flowering smoke.

"No. I wasn't," I admitted. "A bet? I didn't know you were a gambling man."

"It's a sure thing," he said. "I can't lose, but you won't think so and that's why I can make it."

"What do you mean?" I sat forward in my chair. My scalp tingled.

"Your wife," Robert said. "The wager is your wife."

I stared at him. I knew that whatever it was I

would go along with it. It was too late. I was too far out into the bog to get back out. So, I forced a laugh.

"My wife?" I asked.

"Yes."

I laughed again and said, "What do you mean?" I took another puff of the cigar and smiled. I was amazed, afraid, insulted, and eager.

"I just love that red-haired pussy." Now it was Robert's turn to laugh.

I kept smiling. My insides were jelly. I was caught. I would do it. I would do it for the thrill of bathing myself in decadence. I excused it easily enough; it would prove that Robert was not as infallible as he thought he was, my wife would never—would she?

Robert didn't wait for a response, "You want to know more, don't you?"

"Yes. Tell me." I tried a sneer, as if contemptuous of the whole idea.

"I bet ten thousand dollars I can screw your wife. More than that, that I can take her away from you," Robert said. "That may seem a bit cheap for a wife like yours, but half the value of a bet is the thrill of it...don't you agree?"

"Yes." I didn't as much as blink. I already felt the thrill. The intentional wallow in squalor. How would he do it? Or try to do it, because, as I said, I didn't really believe he could. My wife had said more than once she found Robert to be too slick, too perfect, and pompous on top of it. He couldn't carry it off.

"I know what you are thinking," Robert said. "She

loves you too much, right? She would never do such a thing because she is so much in love with her husband."

"I think so." I meant it. She did love me too much to give way to another man; a man she didn't even like, I was sure of it...

"You haven't learned that a woman in love is, in fact, the easiest kind to get? Women who fall deeply in love with one man will more easily fall in love with another. They have a propensity for it. They are the kind of women whose emotions are forever in reach and easily touched. She'll flutter into my arms."

I started to speak out in Cheryl's defense, but Robert stopped me.

"So, you will not take the chance. You will hide behind your indignation. It appears that all our time together has been for nothing." Robert sneered. His sneer was real.

I would prove him wrong." I am not afraid of you," I stated. "And I trust my wife."

"Good," Robert said. "We have ourselves a bet, then?"

"Yes." The audacity of the thing was too much for me. The decadence was too much. Robert had prepared me too well.

The first time I knew he was actually doing anything to follow through on the bet was a week later. He called me.

"Are you ready?" he asked.

"For what?"

"You know."

I was in our backyard grilling hamburgers like a typical middle-class suburbanite, wearing an apron that said, *Hulk the Chief*, with a picture of the Hulk holding a spatula—a gift from Cheryl.

For a moment, I couldn't speak.

"Well?" Robert pushed.

I cannot forgive myself for what I finally did say. Neither can I excuse the reasons I said it, all the excuses I've already admitted. I was no longer merely under Robert's influence, I was captured by everything he and I loved—that he had taught me that I loved—deception, betrayal, selfish pleasure and defiance, even of God.

"I'm as ready as you are," I said. "What are you going to do?"

"I'm going to pay your wife a little visit."

"When? Are you calling to tell me to be scarce when you come?"

"No need. You won't be there anyway. Aren't you leaving on the fourteenth?" he asked.

I was...my annual training with the Guard. I would be gone a month this year, instead of the usual two weeks, because I was scheduled to transition into a new type of aircraft.

"Yes," I replied.

"For a month," Robert said.

"Yes."

"Good. That will be long enough."

I was gone until the end of July; it turned out to be five weeks. I talked to Cheryl every day by phone and email. But, when I came home she was not at the airport to meet me. Never once in those five weeks had she said a word about anything being wrong. No hint of Robert Ray, she never mentioned him.

Perhaps it was just a joke; insensitive, but yet a joke Robert never intended to act on. Perhaps Robert, as unbelievable as it seemed, had lost his nerve. Perhaps I had dreamed the whole damned business up.

Once, I almost asked Cheryl if she had heard anything from him, but then I would have had to explain why I was expecting the call. Instead, I asked her, "Heard from anybody?"

"No, except my mother. Otherwise, just the usual," Cheryl said.

When I got to our house, nobody was there. It was after dark and the house was lightless and silent. The only thing that seemed alive was the red glow of a digital clock on a shelf in the kitchen. The silence sliced through me, the sound of abandonment.

Where is Cheryl? I already knew the answer—and yet I prayed that it wasn't so.

I called Cheryl's parents in Coral Gables. They had heard nothing from her.

"Well, don't worry about it, I'm sure she's at a friend's house," I said.

"Please let us know," Cheryl's mother said.

"I will," I reassured.

I called our friends. No one knew anything.

"Oh, she's out shopping," someone said. In a sane world I would have known that this could be true, but my world wasn't sane anymore.

While I was dialing another number, a car drove up. There was the silhouette of one person in the car, behind the wheel. A man. I made no move to turn on any lights in the house. The silhouette got out of the car and moved toward the door. I waited for the bell. It was Robert Ray.

"My God," he said. "I've done it! I've done it and I'm damned!"

I couldn't see his face in the darkness. My skin prickled like tips of feathers were running up and down my body. His voice was unrecognizable.

"Give me a drink," he demanded.

I turned on the kitchen light. Yes, of course, it *was* Robert. I brought him a bottle of bourbon and he took my arm and led me to my study, turning on the lights as we went. His hand shook on my arm. The house went from abandoned darkness to blazing with every light Robert could reach; he turned on the lights as if the light was his only hope. He sat in the chair in front of my desk and took a long draw from the bottle.

"I've been all the way down," he said. "I have seen the depths. Would you like to know where those depths are?" He sniggered, like a twelve-year-old telling dirty jokes. A terrified twelve-year-old.

I didn't say anything. I couldn't say *no*, even though part of me wanted to say it. I couldn't even resist with so much as that one pitiful word.

"I've come from Haiti," he said. "And though you have not asked, your wife is dead, or, at least, she might as well be." He looked at me, awaiting my response. I was frozen in equal parts of fear and astonishment, with ice at the center of my whole being.

"I sold her," he continued. "The deal was made at the *Fox Club*, right before your eyes, but you were too busy and too stupid to notice. Then, after you left to play soldier, Cheryl took a little trip with me to Haiti. I turned Haiti into a paradise for her with my glib tongue; I plied her with rum, I told her such delicious tales, all about you, Eddie, and all the good times we had together, and she went first to my bed, or rather *your* bed, the first time was in your house, and then to Haiti.

"Want to know how I did it?" he asked. "What? No answer? Cat got your tongue, you poor thing. Well, to continue my saga, it took the whole of two weeks, a record for me, I think. I can't remember a woman ever taking that long to throw herself into my embrace."

The man was boasting. I sat down in a chair, stupefied by it all, held rigid and inert.

"This isn't a joke, is it?" I asked. I must have said it merely to amuse all the fallen angels and demons of Hell. Robert didn't even bother to answer.

"I told Cheryl everything," Robert said. "Yes, my friend, I told her the truth and how much you enjoyed it all, how enthusiastic you were about our adventures. I spilled every one of the beans, I'm afraid.

"I knew she would go off the rails if she found out about our two-man gang-bangs with the girls from the *Fox*. I took a chance; yes, she might spread the tale on me, too. But what is the risk of worldly ruin compared to a chance to wallow like a pig in mud in the delights of Hell?

"Besides, Satan hates the faint-hearted. So I wagered to myself that she wouldn't. I wagered she would, instead, do the most spiteful thing she could to you; fuck me. And I was right—oh, so right. She's hot isn't she, Eddie? I thought she was going to bounce me off the ceiling.

"Did you know that hate can drive a woman to a man's arms as easily as love? Did you know that, Eddie? And then, I gambled too, that your little spouse would do whatever I wanted if it promised to rip you a new asshole, and off we went of Haiti. To celebrate our new love.

"Tell me, how do you think I could know this? About Cheryl? Do you know, Eddie? How could I take such a chance of having my whole life ruined by your wife? I'll tell you, but you won't believe it. Some days I have to pinch myself to see if it is really true—I am the *Bishop of Hell*. That's right, sir—the Reverend Doctor Robert King Ray, Bishop of the Devil's domains.

"I found that out in Haiti, too. I sold your wife into slavery, whore-slavery—made the deal at *Fox's* and turned her over to the slavers in Haiti—she is going to spend the rest of her days, until they leave her in the streets to starve when she is too battered and old, hopped on drugs in the most exclusive whorehouse in Port au Prince. As I said, she might as well be dead. She won't even know where she is most of the time, the Haitians are expert at turning people into zombies.

"And when I had done all that, Satan told me (gracious Satan) that I was his Bishop of Hell. Ha-ha- ha-ha..." A string of laughter; Robert's mouth gaped open showing the moist red and pink of the inside of his mouth, and the perfection of his white teeth.

"I have come to celebrate with you the joys of the damned," he said. "And listen to this, my boy. Listen—you are my Auxiliary Bishop, my assistant. Yes, I mean it. Straight from the Devil's own mouth. Auxiliary Bishop of Hell. That's your reward, son, your certificate of graduation from the course. Congratulations!" This was followed by another string of half-crazed laughter.

The laughter took Robert like a disease—he couldn't stop. It racked his body, his head thrown back against the chair, his body jerking and quivering until his face turned purple.

Which of us was most insane? Which of us closer to Hell? Which of us most degraded?

I had to kill him. I had to make the laughter stop. I had to cut myself away from him, it would not undo what had been done, but it was the only way I could break the connection.

I stood up from my chair. When I took the first step toward Robert, my hands held out for his throat, his head burst into flames. My hands were singed; shocked, I stepped back and raised my arms to shield my eyes. His head burned in blue and yellow flames from his neck to his coiffured hair, like a mask of fire. Yet, his face didn't consume, it didn't distort, it didn't burn away. It was the Rev. Robert Ray's face, handsome as it had always been, but colored by the red, yellow, and blue flames. No screams, and no more laughter. The flames rose to a foot above his head, the heat permeating the room. Robert looked from behind the mask of flame, staring at me, serene.

I was sick. I vomited on my own feet. I fell to my hands and knees and vomited until dry heaves wracked me. I could see the flashes of fire reflected on the wood floor. I looked up, still on all fours like an animal, and saw Robert sitting upright and still in the chair, the mask of fire surrounding his head, holding a crosier in one hand and wearing a miter. He raised his hand in a gesture of blessing and benediction. I ran away.

That's where I am now; I've run away, left Robert in my house. I am in a motel in Mississippi. I drove all night. I'm in a motel in Mississippi, but I don't know what town.

I am waiting. I don't know what else to do. What is there for me to do? Kill myself? What for? That would merely return me to where I am now—

Auxiliary Bishop of Hell. Isn't that where; what I am? Yes, I'm waiting here for my coronation—my crosier and my miter...

I feel heat around my neck. I gasp in terror. It goes away. I sit on the edge of the bed. My face flushes with heat. My palms fly to my reddened cheeks. My ears feel warm. I look up at the mirror across from the bed, seeing silver streaks of sweat sliding down both my checks. My eyes are red, hot, and scratchy. I rub them. Then I feel a heat that seems to come out of the top of my head, I lay my palm on my scalp. I shiver in terror, until the heat stops. What else can I do? How long will I have to wait? What else can I do?

The Great Nothing

Chris "Irish Goat" Knodel

Krin-ya walked along the border with his father, Krin. They looked out across the Great Nothing and Krin-ya asked, as he often asked his father, what the Nothing was.

His father answered him thus: "The Nothing was a land of plenty. There were beings that lived in balance. Some hunted others, some were themselves hunted. Yet everything had its place. For eons the planet maintained this cyclical pattern. But some creatures evolved. Intellect begot Reason. With Reason, came Man. Man came, and killed everything. Man created the Nothing."

Krin-ya asked, "Are you not a man, Father?"

Krin answered, "No, Son. We are not men such as those that started the Nothing. Their kind are dead as a result of war. We are an enlightened mutation of the Man of Before.

Krin-ya smiled. "I am glad of that. I would hate to think that we could destroy our world."

Krin answered, "Son, we are no better than they. Every successive generation feels its intellectual capacity exceeds the last. We call ourselves enlightened because we haven't yet destroyed ourselves. It will come. Our genetic extinction is inevitable."

Krin-ya asked, now with tears welling, "But why father? Can we not stop the killing by knowing the outcome? Do we not see?"

Krin answered, "We see much that the Man of Before did not. But this clarity will not dissuade us, for our arrogance is great. We consider our intelligence immune to auto-destruction. In that very fallacy, are sown the seeds of our own destruction."

Son and father looked back out into the wasteland. The absolute nothingness spanned to the horizon. Krin-ya reached into his breeches and removed a handkerchief. As he finished shedding tears for the fate of his people, he dried his single compound eye.

The Shut In

✛

R.M. Warren

It was the third time the doorbell rang that evening. Or was it the fourth? In any case, whoever was doing the ringing was disrupting *Gunsmoke*, and the old man had had enough.

"Go away!" he shouted from his easy chair.

The doorbell rang again—tinny and grating. *Damn thing sounds like it's about to crap out like everything else in this house*, the man thought. He made a mental note to tell his son to fix it.

"Go away!" he shouted again.

A moment later the doorbell rang once more.

"Dammit," the man muttered, using his cane for support as he struggled to get up from the chair.

He shuffled his slippered feet across the plush, sea green carpeting, slowly making his way to the front foyer. A glimpse of yellow caught the old man's eye as he noticed a sticky note affixed upon the front door. As he leaned forward to read the handwriting on the note, he was startled by three loud knocks on the other side of the door. After a brief silence, there were three more knocks, causing the note to flutter to the floor.

The old man ignored the knocking and bent down to pick up the note, his knees popping as he stood back up. He fumbled through his empty pockets in search of his reading glasses before realizing that they were hanging from a chain around his neck. He put on the glasses and looked down at the square of paper:

DON'T OPEN THE DOOR

He didn't recognize the handwriting. Who wrote the note? If there was a reason he wasn't supposed to answer the door, he couldn't remember what it was.

Didn't matter.

Whoever was knocking, he wasn't buying. He shoved the note into his pocket.

"I don't want any!" he yelled at the door, tapping it with his cane for emphasis.

He turned around and walked back into the living room, swearing under his breath.

He sank back into his chair and promptly dozed off.

It was less than ten minutes later when the feeble ding of the bell rang once again, jarring the man from his sleep. *Damn thing sounds like it's about to crap out like everything else in this house*, he thought, making a mental note to have his son come by and fix it.

"Go away!"

The doorbell rang again.

The man nearly tripped over the leg of his coffee table as he crossed the living room. Evening had fallen, casting inky shadows across the house. This was the time of day he feared the most, when his confusion and agitation worsened. As he made his way to the front door, he saw a thin figure with spindly arms watching him from the corner. Focusing his eyes, he was relieved when he realized it was just his coat rack, standing tall and empty.

The doorbell rang again, followed a few moments later by three knocks. The man scowled and briefly considered opening the door and giving whoever had disturbed his nap the riot act. But as he reached for the deadbolt with his hand—shaky and liver-spotted—he was struck with a vague sense of dread. Something was telling him not to open the door. *But what if there's more than one? What if another is already in the house?* As the thought entered his mind, he could feel someone watching him from the top of the staircase.

He dropped his hand to his side, began unconsciously tapping his index finger and thumb together, and turned around to look up the stairway. As he did, he saw something move against the floral wallpaper at the top of the steps.

He tentatively approached the staircase, gripped the railing with his free hand, and began the slow climb to the second floor. The steps, precariously littered with stacks of newspaper and unopened mail, creaked under his weight as he ascended. He passed framed photographs of his family, several of them hanging askew. Wife. Mother. Son. Daughter. Wife. Son. Mother. Father. Beautiful. Young. Happy. Wife. Mother. Smiling.

He ran his hand along the wall as he reached the landing, searching for the switch. Finally finding it, he flipped it on, filling the narrow hallway with light. Dead bugs in the light fixture cast tiny, speckled shadows across the wallpaper as if they were feeding on the large, pink, painted flowers. The man made a mental note to have his son come by and clean the light fixture before his wife noticed. She always liked to keep a tidy home.

He opened his bedroom door.

"Elizabeth?" he called out.

There was no answer. He turned on the small bedside lamp. The bed was empty and unmade.

"Elizabeth?" he called out again, this time louder and with more urgency.

There was no answer. He was suddenly gripped with terror. *They've taken her*, he thought. *They were here and they've taken her.*

He shuffled through the narrow space between the bed and the wall to his wife's dresser. The dresser was neatly adorned with photographs.

Mother. Son. Wife. Mother. Father. Son. Father. He reached down and opened the top drawer. It was empty. The smell of cedar singed his nostrils.

He reached down and opened the middle drawer—empty.

The bottom—empty.

"Elizabeth?"

The struggling doorbell echoed up the stairs and down the hall. The man walked over to the window, pulled back the lacy curtain, and looked down. Two dark figures stood on his front steps, silhouetted against the flickering porch light.

He opened the drawer of his bedside table and reached his hand inside, his fingertips searching for the smooth, polished wooden handle of his .38 revolver. It wasn't there. He got on his hands and knees and looked under the bed. Under his pillow. His closet. It was nowhere. His son must have taken it. Just like he took his car keys. *I'll call him*, the man thought. *I'll call him and give him a piece of my mind.*

He was in the kitchen rooting through his empty refrigerator—opening it, rooting, closing, opening, rooting, closing, opening, rooting, and closing—for several minutes before he saw the telephone on the counter and remembered why he had come downstairs into the kitchen in the first place. He picked up the receiver and stared at the numbers on the keypad for a long moment before noticing the sticky note taped to the counter next to the telephone. There was a phone number written on it but the last four numbers were smeared and unreadable by what appeared to be a coffee spill. He dialed the first three digits of the telephone number and then unsuccessfully punched in the last four randomly several times before finally giving up and slamming the phone down.

The clanging of the phone chime was immediately followed by the ringing of the doorbell.

"Go away!" the old man shouted.

The doorbell rang again. It sounded broken. He made a mental note to have his son fix it.

The doorbell rang again.

Making his way to the front door, he saw a thin figure with spindly arms watching him from the corner.

Just the coat rack, standing tall and empty.

He wondered where his coat and hat were. He couldn't remember the last time he had worn them. He couldn't remember the last time he had been outside. He reached for the deadbolt. *No. Don't open the door. They are already here.*

Mother. Father. Son. Wife. The smell of cedar. Missing gun. Spoiled milk. Telephone. Ding-dong. Bugs. Shadows. Gun.

●⸱⸱

He was in the basement, rummaging through a cobwebbed past.

Boxes of toys. Water-stained homework assignments. Tools caked with muddy use.

"What am I doing down here?" he mused. "What am I looking for?"

The thoughts racing through his mind were disturbed by a rustling outside. He looked up at the narrow basement window and, through the dust-covered glass, saw something pass by. Then...

The doorbell.

"They're not going to get us," he said, grabbing a baseball bat he saw protruding through an open box. As he made his way up the basement steps, he caught a glint of metal in the corner. It was long, narrow and black.

He carefully backed down the steps and navigated his way through the water-slogged boxes and plastic crates to the corner of the room. He put down the baseball bat and reached for the shotgun. As he pulled the weapon from the corner, a clinging cobweb stretched thin until finally breaking free. He couldn't remember the last time he had held the shotgun. The steel of the barrel felt cold and reassuring under his fingertips. His son had missed this one. For the first time in many years, the old man felt in control again.

As he made his way up the basement steps, the man's thumping heartbeat was in sync with the banging on the front door.

"Leave us alone," he shouted at the door, raising the shotgun. He cocked both hammers. It was loaded—thank God.

The banging stopped and a cracking sound filled its place. The old man looked over at the window next to his door to see a spidery fracture had appeared in its glass.

Behind the cracked glass a face appeared: red and grinning, with yellow eyes.

The doorbell rang again, followed by laughter.

"They're not going to get us, Elizabeth," he whispered. "They're never going to take us away."

The man pulled the trigger, filling his head with a ringing that would not stop.

He approached the door, splinters of wood jabbing through the bottoms of his slippers and the acrid gun smoke filling his nostrils.

Through the large, round hole in the door he saw the silhouettes of three figures running down the street under the amber lights.

There was another smell beneath the gun smoke. Something sweet and wonderful. It took him back to another time. Son. Wife. Mother. Father. He looked down and saw an orange bag adorned with a smiling jack o' lantern face. Its colorful contents were spilt across his front steps.

"No blood," he said, relieved. "No blood."

He looked back up. The figures were smaller, further away, retreating into the night.

An angel.

A devil.

A ghost.

F***ing Up The Universe

Christa Carmen

"You ou can't drink 'English afternoon tea' in the morning," the barista said to her, his eyes blazing like shards of crystal meth about to ignite. "Do you want to be responsible for fucking up the universe?"

Lena started to laugh before realizing this strange man, a man she had pegged as a teenaged hipster before realizing he was much older, was not smiling. Lena's eyes darted to Charlene, trying to gauge her reaction to the thin, tattooed man's outburst. This was Charlene's neighborhood. She came to 1369 Café in Cambridge just about every morning; perhaps she had more insight into the bizarre man's sense of humor.

Charlene stood unmoving, offering nothing but to furl her top lip into a sneer. Lena turned her attention back to the barista and gave a half-chuckle.

"Really though, I'd like the English afternoon tea and...do you have soymilk?"

For a moment the fire in the crazed-looking man's eyes faded, and in a composed, steady voice he said to her, "Indeed we do have soy, it's over on the side table there."

Then he seemed to remember the reiteration of her first request and his face clouded over, his eyes resuming their previous incandescence.

"But I will *not* make you an English afternoon tea until it's *after twelve PM*." His voice was close to a shout, the quality of it grating and unhinged.

This time Lena narrowed her eyes and returned his hard look. "Okay then, is there anyone behind the counter who is willing to make my order? Perhaps your manager?"

The man's behavior became stranger still. Conflicting emotions raged behind those luminous, violet eyes, and he made as if to back away from the register more than once. Each time he jerked forward again, as if his affronted morals were being challenged by his desire to remain employed.

Charlene nudged Lena to the side, her focus on something beyond the glass-fronted bakery case, and called out, "Jason! Hey!"

Charlene's most recent ex-boyfriend lumbered around the hostile hipster-barista and beamed at the two women. "Hey Char, hey Lena. What's up?"

"Well, Adam Lambert here won't make Lena an English afternoon tea...*because it's not afternoon yet*." She ran her eyes over the bird-like barista with cool detachment, letting him know he was on the verge of being dismissed now that Jason was helping them.

Jason regarded the wisp of a man, appearing to be confused not so much with his refusal to fill the order as he was with his general presence behind the counter.

Knowing Jason, Lena thought, *it was probably the first he'd noticed the man had been hired.*

Jason patted the barista on the shoulder with a genial but absent-minded smack, and Lena snuck another look at him before he slunk to the back of the café. The tattoos snaking down his scrawny arms were brilliantly colored—lime greens and vivid turquoises intermingling with neon orange, and a shade of lavender that matched his eyes. The white-blond, multi-crested pompadour he sported looked like a nest of downy birds huddled against a storm, and his face was as pale as his hair, the cheeks sunken in and the skin craggy in places once marred by acne.

Before he disappeared through the swinging door to the café's tiny kitchen, he turned and mouthed something to her. She would have expected something snippy, his pride wounded by the threat of summoning his manager, but she swore he'd said, "Get the English *Breakfast*, or else."

"I didn't know Jason worked here," Lena said to Charlene, as Charlene sipped from a mug topped with foam. Lena's tea was still too hot to drink. "You guys have only been broken up what, three weeks? Did he get this job to stalk you every morning?"

"Of course not," Charlene said, trading the mug for her cell phone.

Lena waited as Charlene scrolled through page after page, likely Facebook, her eyes straying to the couple at the next table in the conversation's lull. A college-aged male held an angry-volcano of a mug an inch from his face, the steam rising before him in unceasing billows. She watched him take four huge gulps of a beverage that was clearly scalding, yet the man did not flinch, somehow unaffected by the drink's temperature.

Charlene tossed her phone aside and addressed Lena again. "Anyways," she said, "Jason needed a job, so I got him one here. I come here so often I know pretty much everyone, and the manager loves me. Besides, Jason and I agreed to stay friends."

Lena tried to keep from staring at the couple next to them. The man wagged a burned and blistering tongue at his female companion, but the gesture seemed informative only; neither pain nor acute emotion of any kind appeared to drive him.

How odd, Lena thought. She forced herself to resume chatting with Charlene.

"Did you say you know pretty much everyone? Do you know that guy that was waiting on us before you called Jason over? What was that guy's deal?"

"The psycho with the giant hair? I have no idea, I've never seen him before in my life. He must be new. But he was definitely weird." Charlene reached for her phone again, her nails clicking as she scrolled.

"Can you get off that damn thing? And I'm allowed to ask that of you because I deleted the Facebook app from my phone a week ago."

"What? Why would you do that? I get all my news from Facebook," Charlene said.

"Your news? Like, world news? I certainly don't need Facebook for the news, that's what CNN is for. Or an old-fashioned newspaper for that matter."

Charlene did not reply.

Lena continued as if Charlene was listening. "Regardless of your social media addiction, I haven't regretted my decision once." She picked up her tea. The red tag flitted at the end of its string like a downed kite, offering peeks of the embossed gold letters spelling out 'English Afternoon.'

The afternoon blend had steeped long enough to cultivate a robust flavor, and Jason had saved her from dumping cold milk from the sidebar into the brew, making eyes at Charlene over the espresso machine as he steamed soy for Lena. It was a perfect cup of tea. She forced the avian-featured barista from her mind, not wanting him to spoil another moment of her day.

Charlene pushed back her chair then slipped her cell phone into her purse. "I've got to run, got to get to class," she said, giving Lena a one-armed hug while she applied a fresh coat of lip-gloss with her free hand. "Text me later. I'd say shoot me a Facebook message, but you've gone and jumped ship. You'll be back, I can guarantee that."

Lena started to protest, but Charlene was halfway to the exit. She checked her watch. Thursdays she started late at the counseling center and if she left now, she'd have time to swing home and grab the binders she'd forgotten that morning. Her tea still mostly full, she retrieved a to go cup from the side station and transferred the nut-colored liquid to it without spilling a drop. Before she left, she thought she saw a pair of violet eyes boring into her from a crack in the back door. Then the door swung shut. She told herself she'd imagined it.

Lena navigated the streets of Cambridge toward Rutherford Avenue. It would take her no more than twenty minutes to get to Revere, and she relaxed into the drive, alternately sipping tea and fiddling with the radio. There wasn't much traffic, and as she glanced to the left to regard a new bar opening soon, she saw a large golden retriever standing over its owner, who lay on the sidewalk with her hands over her head, wound up in the coils of the leash. Lena's head swiveled as she tried to lay witness to the scene without drifting out of her lane. The dog raised its feathered tail, poised to run. The woman shrieked as she was dragged along the concrete, helpless, at the mercy of the dog's apparent decision to turn the tables and walk her.

"What the hell?" Lena said out loud to the empty car. She checked her side mirror to see if anyone rushed to the woman's aid, but the road had curved, and she could no longer see the woman and her dog-gone-wild.

Jesus, Lena thought. *What a weird day*. She pulled onto RT-1, and almost collided with a large paint truck. Three men in city-issued construction uniforms were repainting the breakdown lines, but there were no cones to protect them from oncoming traffic. Lena veered to the left as far as she could but turned her head toward the opposite window, wanting to give the men a 'what the hell' look. The smell hit her then, an acrid, coppery smell. Rather than guiding the truck over the area needing to be painted, the men manually swiped brushes back and forth, smearing something red and glistening over the pavement. Lena had passed the work site before she could perceive any further detail.

Eyes wide and unblinking, Lena reached for her tea, less appealing now in its tepidity, and pressed her foot down on the accelerator. Before she could reflect on the strange goings-on since leaving 1369

Café, a helicopter swooped into her line of vision. The black aircraft flew at such a low altitude, cars had to fan out in a V around its wake. It hovered a few moments then dropped, vanishing from the cloudless sky.

Lena let out a scream. She strained to see across RT-1 and over the side of Storrow Drive. Had the chopper crashed, or only flown so low she could no longer see it? She flipped the radio to an AM news station, but static filled the car.

"Fuck it," she said, and fished her phone from her purse. With all the crazy shit going on, using her phone while driving shouldn't rate high on the list. She opened the Boston Globe app, then the Herald. She had five bars of service, yet the screens remained blank.

"Come on," she said, "Is there a terrorism threat? What the hell is going on?" She ignored the fact that terrorism would explain little more than the helicopter sighting, and even that was a stretch. Lena continued to attempt to access the news sources, even hunt-and-pecking for the letters to type them into the address bar, but Safari would not load either webpage. Frustrated, she reloaded Facebook from the app store, puzzled but thankful when it opened instantly.

Someone on Facebook has to be posting about this shit, she thought, but postponed checking her newsfeed in lieu of the new message notification. She did not know the person who'd sent the message, that much was clear. The name was not

English, but consisted of a set of ancient symbols Lena was certain did not exist on any modern keyboard. When she was able to take her eyes off the road again and review the profile photo, she froze. It was not possible...

Lena had paid for her tea with cash and couldn't conceive of how the hipster barista could know her name, but somehow he'd found her. The message was short, just one line: "Are you regretting your decision yet?"

Up ahead, the tunnel to enter the Tobin Bridge yawned before her, and she felt her hands slip on the wheel in their clamminess. Dread saturated every muscle at the prospect of entering the tunnel and crossing the Mystic River while the knowledge of what was going on still eluded her, but there was nowhere to go but forward. Lena traversed the enclosed section of the bridge without trouble, but relief proved premature. A rumbling had started, faint but audible, and for a moment Lena thought the helicopter was back. She looked into the vast expanse of open air on either side of the bridge, but saw nothing. It was when she checked her rearview mirror that she discovered the source of the rumbling, and it was not the returning aircraft.

Like a scene from a blockbuster action film, the Tobin disintegrated behind her, the Boston side of the bridge breaking off in chunks, showering the surface of the Mystic like gargantuan raindrops. Lena's face blanched and she began to hyperventilate, but she slammed the pedal to the floor and attempted to outrun the destruction. Three quarters of the way over she saw flecks of color glinting in the sun, peppering the falling debris. The vehicles on the first half of the bridge had joined in the bridge's plummeting return to earth.

Her vision narrowed into a tunnel not unlike the one from which she'd just escaped, but just when Lena was certain she'd pass out from the panic, she was over the bridge, the south side of Chelsea whizzing by. Noiseless tears streaked down her face. She felt like she'd tried to swallow a spoonful of cinnamon. She groped for the cup of tea, now as cold as the blood in her veins, and doused the desert that was her mouth, choking slightly, spitting a few drops of liquid onto the inside of the windshield.

She did not remember the rest of the drive to Revere, but her heart only stopped its imitation of a moth beating itself against the glass walls of its lantern prison when she pulled off the exit for Overlook Ridge. The left-hand turn to her complex a mere three hundred feet away, she almost relaxed, approaching a police car with a black pickup truck pulled over in front of it. The driver of the pickup was standing next to a police officer who leaned against the hood of the cruiser and...

Lena jerked forward in her seat and stared. Even with everything she'd seen, even amongst the mayhem and the horror and the apparent breakdown of society, the sight of the pickup driver aiding a police officer in tying off and injecting a syringe in the crook of his arm left her flabbergasted. She did not comprehend the sound of her own muttering, but as she pulled onto Terrace Road, past the red-rocked cliffs of the quarry that skirted her complex, she repeated to herself, "There's no place like home, there's no place like home."

The first building of the complex was the same as it'd always been. The tan and burnt-orange brick fortress blocked the identical second set of apartments behind it, but Lena continued up the winding road, focused only on making it to the third building — her building.

But something was wrong. The second building should have blocked her building from view as the first building had blocked the second. Instead, a monstrously peaked black roof pitchforked up into the sky, no longer cloudless now, but dark and growing darker. As Lena hugged the last curve, and the third building came fully into view, the tea in her stomach soured and confusion muddied her already-taxed brain.

Gone was the impeccably landscaped front yard and walkway, replaced by looming rock structures, grey, dismal, and connected to one another by thick iron chains. Black mud and fissures of wet earth gurgled in the mist, and the great-winged shadow of a vulture moved across the ground in the last of the dying sunlight. The building itself was a castle straight from Hell; any nightmare that manufactured that structure would have been banished to the dreamer's subconscious, never to see the light of day. Its roofline was like a tortured soul, carved and gutted and pierced into things it should never have been. Two lights blazed in twin windows above a horrible pit of a door, their luminescence glowing purple against an otherwise colorless world.

Lena's car moved through the gate and toward that hellish front door through no doing of her own. As the car slowed to a stop in front of it, the air inside the car became unbreathable, suddenly thick and too cloying to move in and out of her lungs. She threw herself from the car, trembling violently as her feet sunk into the black mud.

The infernal door opened with a hideous groan, like the sound of a hundred bones breaking under diseased skin, and Lena could not avert her eyes. She heard the footsteps before she saw him, the vibrant colors of his tattoos now a single shade of blood red, his hair white, his clothes black, his eyes violet.

"I told you," he said, each word taking the same amount of time to utter as the one that preceded it. "But you wouldn't listen to me. I told you you'd be responsible for fucking up the universe."

He Camps Alone

Bruce H. Markuson

"Alright, here's the address of Jack's mother's house," I said after three days of driving. I pulled the car over.

"John, are you sure you want to do this? He hasn't returned any of your calls," Bill said to me from the passenger seat, running his fingers through his army crew cut.

"Look, I'm worried about him. He just hasn't been the same since we got back from Afghanistan."

"You think he might have P.T.S.D.?"

"That's a good possibility. We all saw some heavy fighting over there. Nothing would be better for him than talking to a couple of old army buddies." I told Bill as I opened the door of the car.

We knocked on the door of the nineteen-fifties ranch house as we kicked snow off our boots.

A gray haired elderly lady in an old fashioned dress answered.

"Mrs. Nelson, hi, may I introduce myself? I'm John Baxter and this is Bill Pearson. We served with your son in Afghanistan. We were wondering if he's here?"

"Oh, good. Please come in," she said. "Maybe you can talk some sense into him. He hasn't been acting right ever since he returned from the war."

We stepped into the house and sat down in her living room. An army portrait of Jack hung prominently on the wall. "May we speak to him?"

"He's not here right now. He's out camping."

"Oh. Who is he camping with?"

"He camps alone."

"Alone in the winter?" I asked.

"Yes, ever since he returned back from army survival training in eastern Europe he has been going camping once a month."

"Well, do you know where he is?"

She grabbed a map and circled a point.

"Mrs. Nelson, that's way in the middle of the national forest. He's out in the middle of nowhere."

She answered, "Once a month he checks the calendar, then hops on his motorcycle and goes. It's the strangest thing."

"Mrs. Nelson, is he okay?"

"No, and he's not seeking any help."

"Tell you what, Mrs. Nelson, maybe we will go up

there and visit him."

"That might do him some good."

Bill and I were prepared. We had camping equipment in my car for this road trip to Jack's house. We took a long and lonely drive to the woods. We checked the map as we passed a tavern on the road and continued driving.

After a few miles I slowed the vehicle. "Right there on the side of the road...that's his motorcycle. How could he carry any camping equipment on that little thing?"

Bill and I strapped on our backpacks. It was late at night. Snow drifted in the cold wind through that dark forest. We grabbed our flashlights and I loaded my revolver.

"A .44 Magnum? What do you need that for?" Bill asked.

"Just incase we see bears or wolves. Come on, let's go."

We started following Jack's footprints in the snow.

"Look right here," I said. "Shoes and socks, his coat, he took them off in the cold."

Bill and I were starting to get worried.

"What do you think is wrong with him? Do you think he finally snapped?" I asked Bill.

"I wouldn't put it past him. We need to find him before he freezes to death."

"I agree," I said as we followed his bare footprints in the snow.

"The prints follow the trail along the cliffs," I

added.

Bill and I looked over the cliffs. I realized I should have kept in contact with him; I should have helped him more. We were looking down the cliffs expecting the worst, when all of a sudden, Bill said to me, "Right over there."

In the shadow of the trees we saw a figure wearing a pair of torn jeans and a tattered shirt eating off of a deer carcass.

"That's it. He snapped."

Bill walked ahead of me. "Jack! Jack! Stop eating that! You'll get sick."

Jack turned to Bill. His face was fur covered and elongated into the snout of a wolf.

"Jack?" Bill said. It was too late. Jack jumped on Bill and ripped his throat out. Blood dripped from Jack's fangs as he stared at me.

"Jack, is that you?" I screamed as he came toward me. I ran down the cliff path but he was catching up to me. I drew out my revolver and shot.

BOOM!

Jack jerked back then continued forward.

BOOM! BOOM! BOOM!

I shot him over and over in the chest. Again he jerked back, slowing down a bit. I ran along the cliff, turned a sharp corner, and found a spot. I waited for a moment. Then he appeared.

BOOM!

Climbing down the cliff side I sought a solid foothold on a protruding rock. I stood three feet below the cliff's edge and waited. I grasped onto the cold, moss covered wet stone. I was sure this was the end as the night wind blew against me.

My hand was trembling with fear. Despite all that I'd been through in Afghanistan, I had never before faced an enemy who couldn't die.

After a moment, I heard a low growl. I smelled the odor of rotting flesh on his hot breath. Drops of blood and drool struck me on the forehead. Jack was climbing down the cliff toward me.

"One shot, one shot left." I reminded myself as I squeezed the trigger.

BOOM!

The bullet found its mark, right between the eyes. The creature's head snapped back. Jack struggled frantically pawing at the stone face of the cliff. His clawed grip was lost as he fell into the darkness.

Panicked, I ran back to the car as a sickly howling from that wounded beast echoed throughout the bottom of the ravine.

•..•

"Once a month, during the full moon," I muttered to myself, sitting at the tavern Bill and I had passed the day before. I drank from a bottle of scotch trying to think about what I was going to tell the police. Then I heard a chair being pulled out at my table.

"Jack," I muttered.

He had the same torn jeans and under his coat his tattered shirt, now with six bullet holes in it. He no longer had the elongated wolf face.

"Hi, John. Long time no see. I saw your car in front of the bar. I've been fighting my demons for too long," he said. He held out his hand over the table and dropped six cartridges—.44 Magnum reloads with homemade casted bright silver tips for bullets.

All he said to me was, "Next time."

What Sage Grew

Renee Blue

My lungs are on fire. My legs feel like they are breaking under my weight. Each step feels like an anchor is trying to keep me tethered to the earth. My body is failing to keep me upright through the exhaustion. I collide with the ground. It is sodden and unforgiving as it covers me in mud. I desperately attempt to crawl but my arms can't drag me along. I know what comes next and brace myself.

Boots splash through wet leaves, crunching twigs from behind me. All I can do is roll to look up at the sky. My heart is pounding in my ears as rain falls down my features. I try to implant this moment in my memories. The sound of boot-steps is replaced with heavy breathing at my feet. A large set of fingers tightly grips my ankle, dragging me closer to them. I do not stare this person in the face nor do I respond when they yell at me to stand. I want so badly to cry out. I do not give them the satisfaction of seeing my pain as I am lifted from the ground and bluntly shoved forward. I remain still until the barrel of a gun is pressed in between my shoulder blades. I trudge along, the figure behind me preparing itself incase I run or protest. I decide to submit. I don't want to find out what else they might do to me.

They put me in a clean, dry, black uniform but it is for their convenience—not my comfort. They make me stand naked and handcuffed while their disgusted, judgmental eyes make sure I don't move while they replace my destroyed uniform. There is little compassion here.

My wrists are tightly handcuffed to a bar in an otherwise seamless room. There are two voices conversing. My heart beating and their words are the only noises I can pick up.

"Is the body harmed?" Someone asks the one who brought me here.

"No, just minor abrasions," they respond.

"How are the fetuses?" The first voice asks, no emotion or concern in its tone.

"Healthy, twelve weeks."

I look down at my abdomen. I cringe as I remember how it happened.

They brought me to The Room—red walls, a large mattress and silk sheets. They always told me to remember that I am saving our kind.

I was bound to the metal frame when a large man walked in. The man didn't speak, they never did. Sometimes they were dressed like me and sometimes they wore business suits or clean seamed attire. I was never given a choice. It took a few times of rebellion to find out what happens to those who fight back. I closed my eyes and imagined anything else. The worst times I pictured death. Thirteen children, five years. I was so close this time. I was almost free...

Amidst the white walls I am a black mass. The fabric I am wearing is too big, too heavy. My knees are pressed against my chest, prepared for whatever may come next. The wall directly in front of me opens. A doctor comes in and walks quickly toward me releasing the handcuffs. I recoil when the metal falls to the floor.

"Stand," the doctor orders. I obey and follow the doctor out of the room and down a hall. White walls. White floor. White ceiling. White everything. We walk into a room with shelves covering every inch of the walls. They are stacked with clear boxes filled with medical supplies of varying uses. Everything is sterile, crisp and sharp. It seems just by opening your eyes you'd get cut. I am told to sit in the only chair in the middle of the room. The leather feels like ice beneath my skin. I feel exposed.

I am forcefully leaned back. My shirt is pulled up and a jelly is spread onto my stomach. A wand is pressed into the jelly—one end has a scanner, the other a small screen. The doctor's face remains still and unemotional as they take pictures and clean off my abdomen. Everything is done in silence and with extreme efficiency. They walk over to a shelf pulling down two boxes, which they bring toward where I'm sitting. They pull out two marble sized balls.

"These are density spheres, they have the density of a bowling ball," they explain condescendingly. "There is no running if these are attached to your ankles, so don't try."

They shackle two metal bars around my ankles, clipping the spheres to either anklet with a chain. My legs immediately start dangling over the chair's edge before the weight is too much. I allow them to drop against the linoleum.

"You should know what this is," the doctor says, pulling a small sensor bead from one of the boxes. It is no bigger than a corn kernel. The doctor drops the bead into an injection gun and lifts up the side of my shirt to reveal skin that is littered with small gash scars.

"They made this new model just for you," they state. They push my sleeve down and before I can piece together that this sensor will be going somewhere new, they look me straight in the eyes and stab my side, injecting the sensor. I wince, noticing the slight smirk on the doctor's face. I can feel the small device has left a bump under my skin. This one has been made to keep me from getting it out.

The doctor reaches into their pocket and pulls out a remote with only one button on it. I can already tell what makes this one special. When the gloved finger presses down on the button, a sharp pain spreads and blood runs down my side. Tendrils released from the sensor are moving under my skin, latching onto anything to keep me from being able to dig it out easily. The doctor wraps a bandage around my torso and starts putting away boxes. Sensors were created to store the body's information over time. Anything from hormone changes, to calorie intake, fetal development or nutrient deficiencies is scanned and put into the sensor to be accessible to doctors in a close enough range. They were made to replace camera monitoring, giving the illusion of privacy.

"You are free to head to your room," the doctor decides.

I slide off the chair nearly collapsing, the mass from the spheres planting my feet. My legs strain as I drag them out of the room into the white halls. At one end there is a large black door guarded and locked. The other end there is nothing but a row of doors with only one way out. The only times I leave this hall is on the way to delivery—it is the first layer of many guarded doors made to keep everything inside. They have put no cameras in this hall besides those facing that door, relying only on the sensor to parole me. They are confident in their technology and can know everything they need to in this way.

My room is the only door with an engraved label. *Subject #7456,* it says. The numbers are shallow and the metal plate is eroded. It isn't locked so I let the door open entirely. I do not take a step inside. The room is large, no windows. The walls are painted a dark blue and there is a bed placed in the leftmost corner. They've cleaned it since my escape. All of the paint is scrubbed and everything has been replaced.

I step inside the room. The door slowly starts closing itself behind me. A lock clicks. I am secluded. I fight the hopelessness and will myself to trust that I will not die here.

I head toward the mattress. Next to it is a small table where a book and pencil lie. I pick them up and do the one thing I still have for myself: writing. I had learned to write before the Great Barren, before I was taken here, before they stopped letting me know anything. I start with what I know, or at least what I remember...

My name is Sage.

I am Subject #7456.

I am not barren.

The sky is blue and grass is green.

The human species is dying.

I am expected to help keep it living.

I escaped because I outsmarted their technology.

I had a father.
I don't remember what he looks like.
I may have been wiped of some memories.
I was brought here when I was twelve.
I have been here for five years.
I am not sure if I will get another chance to run.
I do not know where I'd go if I did.
I will not die here.

I erase that last one four times until I finally decide that it deserves to be there. Even if I'm not sure how to make it a reality.

I think of the Great Barren. The reason I am here, the reason none of the lives I've had inside of my body will ever know who I am. They will never know the pain I was put through just so their lungs could taste air. My body is owned by the government now.

Overpopulation was to be fixed by creating a toxin to disrupt the reproduction abilities of any sexually mature human being. It was undetectable in labs analyzing food and was spread throughout the country's food system. Less children were born, less marriages stayed together, but it was subtle. Decades passed and other countries began utilizing the toxin until it was out of control. In thirty years the world's population was reduced by one-fourth. Fifty years it was in half. People gave up, infidelity was common. The children that managed to be born often were infertile. The human race still wasn't aware of why their bodies were no longer working. Seventy years and humans are no longer a thriving species. World governments searched for the few who could reproduce. These people would disappear from their homes in the middle of the night—no one could find where they were taken.

I don't not remember how I got here. The seven thousand four hundred and fifty five before me were immune, as I am. Each one helped to create a stronger toxin that only the government could control. Many of those before me have died from old age, suicide, giving birth. I am considered 'lucky'. I am alive after they had perfected the process of using people like machines.

Now, I am quarantined here. Many have come in and used my body like a factory for children. I have remained silent as my abdomen gets examined, injected, and I've watched as it expands. Parasites are allowed to grow inside of me. They've destroyed my skin, they've attacked my bones and moved among my organs. Because of them I am weak. Those of us that are left are told we are 'saving humanity'. That may be true but where are the people that are supposed to save us?

I never know what time of day it is when I am here. There are no windows anywhere in this container. I never get to see the earth. I think back to when I escaped. The smell, feel and sound of the rain felt like an intoxicating dream that awakened my senses. Now I only feel broken. They say the fetuses are about twenty-eight weeks, healthy as my aches grow. I should be grateful. They have limited my womb to only two occupants at a time. Many had died during or recovering from the birth of many more at once. They perfected test tube fertilization years ago, but only after did they realize the most efficient births are those where the subjects survived and had minimal recovery time. They stuck with the traditional way of creating the humans, but then used their biologists to double the embryos. *"A perfect system built with efficiency and order"*, they say.

I find myself sleeping less and longing for more. Resting, walking, and simply standing become increasingly less comfortable. I grab my notebook still beside my bed and open it, staring at how crowded it's gotten. I turn to a clean page, my pencil shaky in my hand. I can't come up with a clear place to start so I just let my hand write *freedom.* I write about blue, the moments that seem so far before I was here, the time I escaped and only failed because they made sure I wasn't strong enough to succeed. I write about the air, how it was alive and moving. Here the air is not a luxury but only around because it's necessary. It hurts your nose when you're not used to it, and it is always buzzing like it is being made as you inhale.

For once, I dare to write about the disgust I feel toward what lives inside of me. I question if they'll have feelings, if they'll be like me, if they'll be worth my pain for someone else to be able to sleep at night. I wonder why they must hurt me and if they know how they got there. Do they know how they're born? Do they feel remorse? Are they aware of my feelings? I don't know much about what is going on inside me...

As I continue on this thought path, it turns sour. What if they are hurting me because I deserve it? Maybe I have done something to them that I don't remember. What if I should apologize to them? I can't help but feel guilty as tears start to leave dark marks on the clothes that are struggling to cover my swollen stomach. Almost as a response, I feel the pressure of a body part poking me. I'm taken aback by the feeling because for once it does not seem malicious. For once, it feels gentle.

My blue walls are becoming blurry. I am so fatigued I don't attempt to focus them. I let the walls lull me to sleep, tears adding weight to my eyes. This time the parasites tell me their names in my dreams.

The visits from doctors have become more frequent in the last few days. They tell me they don't want me moving a lot and have stopped expecting me to walk to the examination room everyday. They even took the density spheres off of my ankles. I am going to be delivering within the next few weeks. It has been thirty-two they say, though I had personally stopped counting. They have made sure I will go to term and that everything will be on schedule.

I'm sitting up on my mattress against the wall when I hear the door unlock and watch as a doctor rolls in a cart. I do not look into their eyes. I merely wait until I am spoken to.

"May I have your arm please?" the voice asks, a hand extended in my direction.

I raise my arm and brace myself for the harsh grip but am surprised to find these hands to be gentle. Every movement is delicate and careful as if they're afraid I am made of glass. The doctor wraps a band around my arm to check my blood pressure, constantly glancing at me to verify that I'm in no pain. I can't help but be struck confused by this treatment. I have done nothing to deserve such kindness.

"Are you nervous?" he asks.

I am reluctant to answer, unsure if he is expecting one.

"You're allowed to speak. You can speak, correct?" His eyes grow somber at the thought of me being unable to speak. I am fearful that after so long in silence I may have forgotten.

"No," my voice catches, it sounds odd and I am pleased to hear it after so long. "This isn't the first time. Do you believe I should be nervous?"

The doctor stares at me wide eyed and terror grows in me. I shouldn't have said anything. He gains back his composure before continuing.

"No, you look beaut..." he stops himself. "Fine. You look fine, everything looks fine."

This person talks unlike what I'm used to. It

puzzles me.

"I don't understand. Is there something wrong?" I look at him hoping for some explanation. He appears flustered and begins to organize everything on the cart, moments from leaving.

"Do not worry. You're safe." He is rushing out of the room now and before the door locks I hear the same voice whisper, "I will be back for you, Sage."

This man knew my name even when I had started to forget what it sounded like. His voice reminds me of before all of this, when people's words weren't so cruel. His hands were so gentle, despite being worn down. His eyes were old, unlike the doctors who've checked me before. This man shouldn't be here...but they don't know that.

Everyday I would wait for that man to walk through my door. I counted down the minutes until a doctor visit but *he* hadn't come back...not yet. My belly is still growing rapidly. Regular doctors would come in to do more in depth check ups than what a scanner could tell them. No one mentioned *him* or asked. I started to believe that he had been found or killed.

It is halfway through the second week, yet today the man comes walking through the door quietly. He looks at me and smiles. I smile back without realizing it. It feels good to smile. It has been so foreign.

"Happy to see me?" he asks looking down from my eyes to the cart full of supplies. I hadn't noticed before that his eyes look very familiar—like someone I've seen before. I push that thought away because I have questions he may be able to answer.

"Yes, but I have questions."

His face goes from jovial to stone when I say this.

"I will answer what I can." He is focused on only me now, his eyes solid on mine.

"I know you aren't a doctor," I say. "Why are you here?"

He seems dumbfounded but leans in close as if to tell me a secret.

"I am here to save you from this place," he whispers.

My heart starts to pound in my chest at the thought of freedom.

"But how?" my voice breaks. I am overcome with fear and happiness. "There's only one way out and I can't walk easily."

"Do not worry. I have it all figured out. All you have to do is have the babies and I'll take care of the rest."

I am skeptical but I choose to trust him. I have never heard the parasites referred to as babies but I don't inquire...I have more pressing questions. He has been nice to me and I don't feel I deserve it. I'm trusting he will not hurt me.

"Who are you?"

His eyes become heavy and somber when I ask this.

"I'll explain it all later. I promise, just not here. Not

now." He calms me. Something about this man makes me feel safe.

A tear escapes from his eyes and I feel sorry. I'm not sure as to why but I don't get the opportunity to ease him before he is heading for the door.

"I'll see you soon," his voice chokes as I silently watch him walk out. I worry for the future and what it holds now as I sit alone in my room counting the days until I am relieved of this pain.

Since the man has left I've been writing about his use of the word, 'babies'. I know this word, though I have not heard it in a long time. I remember what babies were—small and loud, yet innocent and gentle. I think of the still growing life inside me and I let myself call them babies. Children. Humans. They only want to live as I do. They are innocent of crime despite my pain. I believe they must not know what they do to me.

I put my hands on my stomach and feel my skin move toward it. Though they do not know it, they still have taken my strength and for that I am hesitant to trust them. I do not know who they will end up being, but I believe they may be worthy of at least being human.

Today I deliver. Usually I dread this day but my heart flutters with nervous energy. I am ignorant to the plan though I am confident in the man who was kind to me.

Two doctors come in to get me towing a rolling

bed with them. I am told to get onto it and comply, then I'm briskly rolled to delivery. White halls pass by as we head to the large guarded door. A doctor types the code to unlock the heavy door, then we are on the move again.

On the other side of the door it is no longer white, but rather grey, and has more rooms with worn down plaques. I am pushed so quickly that when we pass the giant window right before the delivery room, I do not get to admire the outside.

This area is the most dreadful.

I go through all of the motions in my head in the order they will happen. My sensor's live feed getting projected onto the left wall is first. They then have me lie back in a recliner and tell me to not touch any of the many utensils on the surrounding carts. This is where the waiting starts.

There is a constant stream of people coming in and checking on me. At one point they numb my entire lower half by sticking a needle into my spine. The sensor feed so far has been silent, no imperfections, everything is on schedule. I know it's show time when I see the familiar man's face come into the room. The doctor's stop coming in. There is only the man and one nurse here to monitor the progress. The moment I am told to push by the man's soothing voice, I know this is the end. This will be the last time I am forced to do this.

I hear two cries. Normally, this is the time where I

fall weak and exhausted and the infants are whisked from the room. I never get to see them. But today the crying continues.

I lift my tired eyelids open and find the nurse cleaning pink skin on squirming bodies. The man in his long, white, lab coat is standing over the nurse's shoulder keeping a close eye. He turns around and looks at me, walking in my direction.

"Two girls," he has a wide grin on his face. "Would you like to see them before we leave?"

"Leave? I don't know if I can walk," my voice is groggy.

"Don't worry, I know you're exhausted. You did wonderful," he seems anxious. He looks back at the nurse, who is holding two wrapped bundles in her arms.

"We have to go," the nurse urges.

He nods in agreement. "Let me help you up," he walks over to roll a chair with wheels next to my recliner. "Take my hand."

My limbs are heavy but I reach out, mustering all the strength I can to stand up and move to the chair.

"Can you handle carrying the girls until we get outside?" he questions the nurse, who nods and proceeds out the delivery room.

We follow behind, the man is pushing me quickly down a hall as I struggle to stay awake. There are no guards, no doctors, no one stopping us. The nurse slips a card in the readers of the multiple doors we pass through. We are moving fast. I am unnerved by how silent and vacant the institute is. Has something happened?

I am wheeled into an apartment I recognize. This is the last door before we are outside. There are no fences or walls around the large building. They have always been so sure, I, nor anyone else, would ever escape again.

"This is as far as I can go. I must stay behind and cover so you can get as far away as possible," the nurse's small voice says to the man.

"I can't hold the babies and push you at the same time," the man tells me, concern is evident.

"I think I can hold them." I am surprised to hear the words but I trust my body to know what to do. A burst of adrenaline and nerves go through me. Exhaustion starts to die down. The nurse bends over putting a girl in each arm. Only their faces are visible.

The man whispers a, 'thank you' so sincere as he takes the lab coat off and hands it to the nurse. The nurse scans an ID card once more and the final door creaks open. Air rushes in washing over my skin. I take a large breath in, overwhelmed with emotion.

The man pushes me outside. I look down at the life in my arms, not paying attention to where he is taking me. I notice the ground beneath me get bumpier as the man struggles to push me across the dense forest floor.

The girls are so small. Their skin is pink, their eyes are shut. I can feel their little breaths through the blankets swaddling them. I see them as babies, not as parasites. This is the first time I've gotten to witness what was growing inside of me for months. I can't keep my eyes away. One of them yawns and her eyes open for a moment. Beautiful grey eyes shine up at me. It is too much to handle. Tears fall down my face, but I smile.

"I am so sorry," I breathe. I hope I am forgiven for all the hate I had. Nothing this innocent could be to blame for my suffering. They are babies, they are humans, they could not have known.

We stop far into the forest. That horrendous building is no longer in view. In front of me is a dark blue truck.

"This will take us the rest of the way," the man's heavy breath says. He rolls me to a door, opens it and helps me stand. It is easier this time. I climb inside with the babies still safe in my arms. The truck is loud as it starts up but the babies don't seem to mind. As we accelerate, my energy finally begins to calm and balance. Within moments, I am asleep with babies in my arms and the man who rescued me at my side...

The sun is sitting on my eyelids when I finally wake up. I try and remember what happened—a nurse, two girls, grey eyes, a dark blue truck and the forest. I have no idea where I am and I have no idea where the babies are.

My eyes shoot open. I sit up quickly, the soreness then hits me. I am in a bed with green covers over my lower half. I am wearing faded purple pajamas that are soft and comforting. The room is filled with a wonderful yellow glow. A lump forms in my throat. I am a medley of overwhelmed, relieved and fearful. But I am free, I am safe, I am going to be okay. I glance down at my abdomen seeing that it is no longer swollen. My heart is pounding. I need to know where they are. Where are my girls? Slowly this time, I pull my legs over the edge of the bed, testing my feet's strength. Standing isn't comfortable but it is bearable. I take a deep breath and convince myself to leave the warmth of the room.

There is a handle on the inside of the door. It isn't locked. I am free to move as I please. This forgotten feeling brings a smile to my face. I walk from the room, a mission set in my head of finding the babies. I explore the area, then I hear faint voices coming from downstairs. I am hesitant of everything I see—there is so much I don't remember from before I was twelve, so much of it got lost in the solitude.

"...Charles don't worry...can't I just hold..." this voice is higher. I do not recognize it. The conversation gets clearer as I carefully step down the stairs.

"No, wait until their mother wakes up. Be respectful." This time it's a deeper voice.

I step off the last stair and turn to find myself in front of the two people I heard talking. It is the man who helped me escape and a small woman with skin as dark as ink and hair tightly coiled like wire.

"Good morning, Sage," the man greets me with a smile. "I'm sure you have questions. I'm here to answer them."

"Where are they?" I assert more harshly than intended.

The man simply points to a crib on the other end of the room. I run over to it, immediately relieved at the sight of my two babies asleep and present.

"We made sure they were safe and happy. We wanted to let you sleep as long as you needed to," the woman assures.

"Thank you." I pause and take a breath. "Who am I thanking exactly?"

"My name is Charles," the man responds.

"And I'm Victoria," adds the woman.

"Do you remember me at all?" Charles eyes me hopefully.

"You remind me of someone I've seen before. But I am sorry, I do not," I divulge.

His demeanor changes. I worry I may have said something wrong.

"That's alright. They may have tried to dull your memories," his voice catches. "No use in hiding it. You used to call me, 'daddy'. I tried to save you before, I really did."

This news is surprising but it makes sense. In this moment I wish I knew what to say. I wish I could return the love this man must feel for me. I watch as his eyes start to sparkle. I am compelled to embrace him.

"I may not remember much of who you were before, but you saved me now and for that I am more grateful than I can express," I voice into his chest.

"I don't want this to be a sad day," he announces to Victoria and I.

"You're right," Victoria agrees. "We have three new members of our family today. We should celebrate!"

I nod in approval. We all move to stand above their crib. I say each one's name as I'd heard it in my dream. Incredibly, their eyes open in response. I can't even think back to the life where these babies were anything less than people. I am never leaving their sides.

The Growl

✠

S. Rey

It was the day before Halloween, the weather
damp and dreary. I was driving down a dark road
on my way home. Just me and my pit bull, Sweet
Sandy. We were beginning to tire from a long day
of play at our favorite dog park, when the rain
came, pouring sheets of ice-cold rain. Fall was
definitely in the air. Sweet Sandy was in the
passenger seat next to me gazing out the window
as we made our way down a dark, deserted road
headed toward home.

I always preferred to take the scenic route away
from traffic, but was questioning my judgment on
this night. It seemed like the darkness came upon
us suddenly, but with classic rock on the radio and
my best friend at my side, nothing could ruin my

day. That is, until the radio began to fade in and out. Sweet Sandy looked at it with raised eyebrows, curiosity piqued. This didn't concern me much, until I noticed the dashboard lights begin to dim and flicker. Next, it was the headlights. I am no mechanic, but my father loved to work on cars and taught me much of what he knew. The battery was dying, possibly due to the alternator. Just as I began to ease to the side of the road, the car died completely—lights and all. Being that I had chosen to drive the back roads, there were no street lamps or houses to provide any light. Sweet Sandy and I were suddenly shrouded in a thick cloud of darkness deeper than any I could recall. I waited a moment while my eyes adjusted. Sweet Sandy looked at me. I shrugged.

"Guess I'll get out and take a look," I told her as I pulled my hood up over my head and got out. I remembered I had a flashlight in the trunk, and was soon standing drenched under the hood, shining a light on the engine. I did not immediately see any issues, but my experience told me it was an issue with the battery and I needed a jump. Now where in the world was I going to find another car with cables? I know you're thinking, *It's 2016, call someone on your cell!* Well, I guess you could say I'm old fashioned. Especially when it's just me and my dog, I find no need for a phone. I leave it at home often.

I got back in the car. Sweet Sandy looked at me expectantly. I was sure she understood our predicament. This dog was smarter than the 'average bear,' that's for sure.

"Well, Sand, looks like we got ourselves a little problem." As I was speaking to her I noticed her gaze shift. Her eyes moved from mine to something behind me and her demeanor completely changed. She suddenly seemed anxious, as if something had frightened her. I was afraid to turn around, but forced myself to do so. At first I did not see anything. I squinted, and after a moment I noticed a small light that had not been there before. The more I stared at this light, the more I began to make out the details around it. Was it? Yes! It was a house! But where had it come from? Why had I not noticed it before? And why was Sweet Sandy reacting to it in such a way? I had no answers, but frankly it didn't matter. I was not prepared to walk the ten miles back to our house in the rain, and I knew that if not jumper cables, this house would at least have a phone.

"Good girl, Sand," I said giving her a reassuring pet. She lowered her head and looked up at me. I already knew she would not want to accompany me to this mysterious house, but I was not about to leave her here, so she would just have to suck it up.

I opened the door and prepared to sprint. "Come on Sandy!"

She hesitated a moment, but seemed to decide she would rather follow me into the unknown than be left behind in the car. We took off across the road and raced toward the house, rain pelting our faces painfully as we ran. We reached a long gravel driveway with wrought iron gates that looked as though they had not been used in decades. Lucky for us, they were wide open. Suddenly, I realized the light we had been running toward was no longer lit. The house was shrouded in such darkness I could barely make out the outline. The darkness here was not only seen, but also felt.

We made our way up the steps and halted, thankful to be out of the rain. The door was closed. By all appearances this house had been empty for years. But I knew I saw a light. Sweet Sandy saw it, too. There was definitely someone here.

I lifted my fist to knock, and just as my knuckles brazed the wood, the door opened. The darkness inside was more vast and consuming than what was outside. A feeling of dread overtook me.

You shouldn't be here, a voice inside my head warned. I looked down at Sweet Sandy next to my side. She seemed to be sharing that dreadful feeling. I shook it off and peered around the doorframe. I could make out a large foyer directly ahead and a winding staircase off to the left. At the top of the stairs the hall was lit up, although I could not make out any details.

"Hello?" I called loudly, looking toward the top of the stairs. There was no response. I was just about to turn away when Sweet Sandy's ears perked up. I peeked in the house again and heard a voice call to me from upstairs.

"Come in. I'm upstairs," came the voice of what sounded like a young, attractive female. This turn of events was a bit strange, but once I heard that voice I could think of nothing but putting a face to it. I am a man, after all. I could feel Sweet Sandy's gaze upon me as though she could hear my thoughts. I told you, this dog knows much more than she should.

I stepped over the threshold and turned to shut the door, when I realized Sandy was still on the porch.

"Come on girl," I called, to which she did not budge. She made a sound that was part whine, part moan, and planted her butt on the wood. She did not want to come inside—that much was obvious.

"Sandy, come," I said, in as stern a voice as I could muster. With that, she knew the choice was not hers and decided to come. Although she did it slower and with much more caution than I had ever seen from her before.

When we were both through the door, I turned to shut it. As I did, the feeling of dread returned. It felt as though I was shutting the door to reality and stepping into a nightmare. I chuckled to myself and closed the door anyway. Rain, a broken down car, a dark mysterious house and 'All Hallow's Eve' made the perfect recipe for a fright-fest. I knew better than to give in to that nagging fear. Besides, it felt good to be out of the rain, although we were both dripping water all over the floor. I would have to apologize when I met this curious woman waiting for us upstairs.

I started up the curved staircase, Sweet Sandy following behind with her tail tucked between her legs. In any other circumstance I may have been more concerned with her unusual actions, but the woman's voice was reverberating in my head. Calling me up the stairs. She had me so enthralled I did not even notice the cobwebs caked on the banister.

I reached the top landing and saw a dark hallway that did not seem to have an end. There were doors on both sides; some open, some closed. The light was coming from the second door on the right. The first door was closed, as were the two on the left. I had no desire to snoop and went directly toward the light. As we entered the room, a chill came over me. I noticed the temperature was quite a bit cooler here. Although, what bothered me more than the temperature change, was the fact that there was no one here. There was an older looking canopy bed, an armoire and dresser with a small oil lamp burning away on top. In the corner was a full-length oval mirror. The whole room was decorated in paintings, rugs and throws that looked to be outdated by at least a century. This was the moment I realized the cobwebs and dirt I had seen in the foyer and staircase were quite the opposite of this room. This room, was pristine. And yet, I did not see any sign of clothing or any other object that would hint to a resident.

I entered further and immediately felt a pull towards the mirror in the corner. I approached it feeling as though I was walking on legs that were not my own. When I got to the mirror, the reflection I saw was not my own. It was my body, and the general outline of the face seemed to be mine, but the lips were curled in a snarl. A barely parted evil grin revealed many small pointed teeth. The eyes were merely black holes; completely missing any hint of an iris, or pupil, or even an eyelid. I was locked into a staring match with this terrifying face and I could not break away. I began to feel angry. I became full of hatred. My hands tightened into fists as I contemplated punching the reflection. I could see myself smashing the mirror to bits, picking up a piece of the broken glass, and slashing the next person I saw with it.

A low growl escaped my lips and startled me. It only took a moment to realize the growl was not mine. For the first time since looking into the mirror I was able to avert my gaze from the frightening demon. I was able to look beyond those insane eyes to what stood reflected behind me. There stood Sandy, although she did not have her usual sweet composure. She stood behind me, glaring into the mirror. Her hackles were raised, teeth bared, and she was issuing a low menacing growl that I had never known her to be capable of. The incredibly frightening sound of it gave me the jolt I needed to finally turn away from the mirror. Relief washed over me. The relief was not long lived however, when I thought about Sweet Sandy growling.

This growl did not coincide with the beautiful, sweet dog I rescued from the shelter many years ago. Whoever started the rumor that pit bulls are a vicious breed needs to meet Sandy. She is the sweetest animal I have ever known. She would never hurt a fly, a child or even a stuffed toy. She always gave them a place in her bed and treated them with great care. I had never heard a malicious peep from her, and hearing one now frightened me more than I could comprehend. It was then that the first hint of pain escaped my tensely squeezed hands. I had them fisted so tightly the nails had dug into my palms, drawing blood.

When I turned from the mirror, Sweet Sandy came to me and huddled down on the ground. I knelt down and touched my forehead to hers. She had just saved me from something. I am not quite sure what, but that malice was like nothing I had ever felt. I had never wanted to hurt someone the way that I had in that moment. That was not me. Sweet Sandy gave me a forgiving kiss on the cheek. It was then that I loved her more than ever, and I prayed that I never heard that growl again.

"Jaaaacksonnn..." The female voice called again. This time from somewhere deeper in the house. But sweet as it sounded when it called my name, the voice suddenly turned into maniacal laughter, an evil sound that reverberated throughout the house.

"It's time to go Sandy," I said. She did not need more urging. When I crossed the threshold into the hallway, I was shocked even more by the sight I found there. The winding staircase that should have been there was gone. The hallway to the right, now appeared identical to the left; a few feet of light from the oil lamp in the room and then nothing but blackness.

My pulse began to quicken as I realized something was very wrong. How was I going to get out? I looked down, reassured that Sweet Sandy was by my side. She seemed just as confused as I. My mind was speeding toward the first stages of panic, when I felt something that brought me fully to the present. It felt as though a finger was tracing the length of my spine, from the bottom of my skull to the top of my jeans. Someone had just run their hand down my back! My pulse quickened as I whipped around. There was no one there. The line that had been traced suddenly began to burn as though something had set it alight. I frantically groped at my back checking to see if I was being burned alive. When I felt the clothes were dry and cool, I felt my back underneath. My fingers traced a raised tender mark as if I had been gouged with a sharp, menacing claw.

"Jackson!" A whisper in my ear, so close I felt the breath upon my neck. That was all I needed. I began running down the hallway in the direction that the stairs should have been, Sweet Sandy padding along at my side. As we ran, the laughter started again; a sepulchral sounding laugh causing the hairs on my head to stand on end. The sound made me run faster still. The more I ran, the darker it became. When I felt sure that I had run the length of the house and back, I stopped and turned toward the direction I had come. I noticed a dim light far off in the distance, shining from the room with the terrifying mirror.

After my breathing calmed and my heart slowed to the point where I could no longer hear the blood rushing through my head, I looked down at Sandy. She was standing stiff, ears pricked, eyes on something in the darkness behind me. I turned and tried to see what she saw, but with my human sight I could see nothing but blackness. My ears, however did not fail me.

Thud — thud — thud.

I closed my eyes and concentrated on the sound. What was that? I heard it again. Definitely louder this time. My eyes shot open and I stood at the ready. It sounded like boots thudding on the carpet, running toward us. As if the echo of my own boots was still resounding off the walls. Someone, or some THING, was rushing at us.

My heart began to race again. At my side, Sandy raised her hackles and issued the same low warning she had in the bedroom — the growl that I never knew she was capable. My palms began to sweat. I backed against the wall, unsure which way to turn or where to go. I had no desire to see what was running toward us, but found myself frozen in fear. The stomping boots were bearing down on us, closer by the second. Then, the scratch down my back began to burn and it gave me the jump I needed. I took off, running back the way I had come. I rushed past the door with the light. Ahead, I noticed a door on the right standing slightly ajar. Being too scared to simply rush blindly into another room, I slowed and held my breath. Sweet Sandy was panting beside me, but other than her heavy breathing, there was silence. I looked back toward the sound I had previously heard. My eyes strained in the absence of light. There was nothing there. No mysterious runner, and still no staircase. Nothing but darkness.

I needed light. If I was going to go anywhere else in this house, I needed to get that oil lamp. I was scared to death of confronting whatever I saw in the mirror again, but the need to be out of darkness outweighed that fear. I slowly sidestepped my way back toward the bedroom, glancing in every direction, running past each door on the way.

When I reached the bedroom, I covered my peripheral vision with my hand in the direction of the mirror and went straight to the dresser. As I picked up this antique looking oil lamp I noticed that there did not appear to be any oil. It appeared to be burning on its own. I didn't take the time to inspect it. At this point, that was the least profound of all the unexplained phenomena I had dealt with this evening.

I needed to think. I needed to sit for a moment and figure out how to get out of here. But there was not a chance of that happening in this room.

I walked out of the room, again protecting my eyes from the mirror. I walked into the hallway and stopped. Silence. As far as the light from the oil lamp would reach was blackness in either direction. I turned to the left and began to slowly make my way toward the door I had found slightly ajar. With one hand on Sweet Sandy for comfort and one holding the oil lamp high, we reached the door that caught my attention. This door was the only one I had seen that was not open or shut, but somewhere in between.

I locked eyes with Sandy for a boost of confidence and then slowly pushed the door open. It was dark, but not black. The ceilings were vaulted, the windows towering, dwarfing all modern-day windows. Pinned up curtains swept the floor. In the middle of the room sat a grand piano. This room, much like the bedroom, had the appearance that it had been recently occupied. The piano bench was askew. The cover for the keys lifted.

I swallowed hard and went to the window. The moon was shining through and gave the room an eerie, whitish glow. I looked at the sky and noticed there was nothing but stars. The clouds must have passed. I saw no evidence of rain. How long had I been here? I looked down and saw a large grassy knoll leading into a dense forest. It might have been quite beautiful had the circumstances been different. For the first time, I felt my heart slow to an almost normal pace. I would stay here until I could decide what to do next. I found a corner, slid down the wall and set the lamp on the floor next to me. Sweet Sandy came and sat beside me, too alert to lay down. I pressed my forehead into hers, trying to draw comfort from the connection we shared.

"What is going on, Sandy? Where the hell are we? And how do we get out of here?"

She looked me in the eye and rested a paw on my lap. I can't remember ever being this scared before, let alone my Sweet Sandy. There was nothing here to physically harm us, and yet I felt as though we were in grave danger, as though our very lives were at stake. I had to get us out. There had to be a way. Maybe if could just sit for a moment and clear my head. If I was able to slow my breathing, and calm my pounding heart, I may be able to figure a way out of this mess.

I closed my eyes, relaxed my shoulders, and began to slow my racing thoughts. I focused on my breathing.

Breath in. Breath out.

I felt the sweat on my brow begin to dry. I felt Sandy begin to relax next to me. We sat in silence for several minutes.

Then I heard the most wonderful sound. The piano began playing, the sound lulling me into a dream like state. Sweet Sandy suddenly stood and roused me from my state. Someone was playing the piano. Someone was playing the song my mom always played for me! This 'person,' this thing, knew too much about me. I was too afraid to open my eyes, terrified of what I would see. But I could feel the fear rising, feel the malice. Whatever it was, it was not my mother. I opened my eyes and the music stopped. There was nothing there. Sweet Sandy suddenly began to growl again. This time so loud and forceful, it frightened me even more than the eerie piano music. I stood scanning the room, trying to follow her gaze. Trying, and failing, to see what she was seeing. There was nothing there.

Then my Sweet Sandy started barking. A loud, frantic, scared bark. She was terrified and shivering. I attempted to lay a reassuring hand on her when she was suddenly flung about five feet from where I sat. She yelped and flew as if someone had booted her, very similar to punting a football. My sixty-five pound pit bull was just physically attacked by something I could not see!

When she was able to regain her footing she yelped again and took off running.

"Sandy! No!!"

She ran out into the hall and I ran after her. She was too fast. I saw her turn right, but by the time I rounded the corner she was out of sight. I ran as fast as I could, yelling her name. I left the oil lamp behind, but didn't care. I couldn't lose Sandy. I kept running until suddenly I heard her claws clicking on tile as if she had found a new part of the house. The stairs! Could it be? I did not recall seeing tile anywhere else.

I slowed my pace as I neared the clicking sound—barely in time as I reached the top of the staircase. There was a small amount of moonlight shining in through a window downstairs, just enough to reflect off the tiled stairs. I stopped at the top looking for the first step. I still couldn't quite make out each one. As I lifted my foot to begin the descent, I felt two hands on my back; ice-cold hands that caught my breath in my chest and my foot froze in fear. Before I knew it, those hands pushed, and being that I still had one foot in the air I was caught completely off balance and went head first down the stairs.

When they say your life flashes before your eyes, they are not lying. I remembered everything. My mom, my dad, growing up, my schools, my friends, my girlfriends. Flashes of high school and college. Finding my sweet, Sweet Sandy—all in a matter of seconds. Suddenly, there was a fierce blow to my head, blinding pain, and blackness.

I awoke to the sound of the rain pattering against the windows. I did not yet open my eyes as I tried to recall what had just happened and where I was. It didn't take long for it to all come rushing back, and just as it did, my heart filled with dread. I slowly opened my eyes. I was staring at a ceiling, but not a twenty-foot-high ceiling like was in the house. I was somewhere else. I looked to my right.

There sat a nightstand with a green digital clock that read 3:15 am. That was my clock. This was my bed. I was home!

"Sandy!" I yelled.

I sat up quickly and Sweet Sandy raised her head from the end of the bed. There she was, lying in her usual spot down at my feet. She gave my hand a reassuring lick and then laid her head back down. The relief that washed over me was indescribable. It was only a dream! I got out of bed and walked to the bathroom. On the way I passed the boots I had worn the day before and noticed they were covered in mud. A strange recognition gnawed at my subconscious, as if it could explain why, however my muddled, half-asleep brain would not yet let me come to grips with understanding.

I turned on the bathroom light and was immediately hit with a terrible pain in my head. It was pounding. I blinked my eyes, quickly trying to adjust to the light. When I could finally open them fully, I glanced in the mirror. There were huge, dark circles under my eyes. My cheeks were gaunt and there was a large rounded lump where the pain was originating. I looked like I hadn't slept in days.

I took in a sharp breath. The last thing I remembered in my dream was hitting my head while trying to escape in the house. But it was just a dream, wasn't it? It had to have been. I took a few deep breaths, turned out the light and crawled back into bed. Sweet Sandy curled up next to me as if she knew I needed the comfort. I would figure everything out in the morning. For now, I needed sleep.

As my eyelids began to get heavy, I felt Sandy jolt. Suddenly, she issued a low, menacing growl...

The Created Children: The Hidden Workshop

Barbara M. Scanlon

O*ctober 31, 1987*

<u>Evening News</u>: The Richards family has been murdered! Parents and two elder children found chopped into pieces. Five-year-old Fae Richards is missing! Perpetrator believed to be a transient who may have taken the child with him—all points alert!

October 31, 1997

<u>Evening News</u>: Missing teen's body found in Dunger's Pond! Remains of Jimmy Cartmeier, the

captain of Central Valley High's soccer team, found after a large-scale search. Search was initiated when locals discovered severed digits inside fish caught in the popular fishing pond.

October 31, 2002

Evening News: Another local teen has gone missing. Seventeen-year-old Connor Mason joins the list of boys to disappear on the bus ride home from County Community College...

The 5:15pm bus arrived after sundown in October. After a long day of school, followed by extracurricular activities and then more school, it wasn't uncommon for the students in the Central High gifted program to fall asleep on the bus. They would sleep as the old Richards' place grew in the distance and then faded away behind them. If they were lucky, a friend, classmate, or kindly neighbor would wake them when the bus pulled up to their stop. If they were unlucky, they would miss their stop and wake up to see the old Richards' place looming in the distance. The surrounding fields were barren—no one had ever bought the land. The house, from a distance, was in disrepair, but up close one could see that all of the doors and windows were intact. Crows gathered in the yard and bats ranged from the abandoned barn. A pack of stray dogs roamed the property, warding off would-be trespassers.

For those unlucky boys, the darkened sky above the seemingly desolate farm was among the last things they would ever see. The bus driver was deceptively strong. He forced the boys inside the lightless house and down into the cellar. There he left them. But they were not alone...

The room was very still. Connor held his breath and then the shadow entered it. She was lithe and pale—the side effects of spending ones time running around in the darkness. Connor never could tell if her hair was black or brown and he reasoned that it didn't matter. Trevor screamed. His right arm was officially detached from his torso. *Funny...*Connor mused. *It took longer this time*. The last boy, whose name Connor had already forgotten, had lost his left leg in three increments: Foot—Calf—Thigh. The ax had taken each piece off with a single chop. Connor had wondered, at the time, whether or not he would be able to handle an ax as well as she did.

The days before he had been taken, Connor had been a typical teenaged boy. He had gone to school, worked part-time at the mall, and hung out with friends. He came up with excuses to avoid the couple he was living with. Connor had been orphaned when he was nine. He had heard the rumors: that the ancient bus driver was the last living schoolmate of the deranged Richards cousin, who had escaped from the asylum in the next town six months before the 1987 massacre; that the

Richards family had taken Looney Luke in, locking him in the basement, to protect him from recapture; that there was a hidden workshop the police had missed in the cellar of the farmhouse. The book he was reading on the bus was so interesting that he didn't even notice that the driver went right past his corner...

Trevor was the sixth boy that Connor had lived with so far. He knew, from the first of them, that there had been others before him too. He glanced over at Trevor. His blood was pooling around the drain. Her toes were painted in it. Connor wondered if she ever wore shoes. He had never seen her wear shoes. He counted the days since Trevor had arrived: five fingers—removed one at a time, one palm—split in two and then removed the following day, three inches of arm the next day, from just above the elbow yesterday, and now: severed at the shoulder. Ten days. Would this be the last? Would she let him bleed to death this time?

That was always the question. Connor inspected his intact limbs and wondered, when it was his turn, where she would begin. The first boy had said that Connor was special. As he lay there, his spine the only thing left holding his torso to his waist, he said that Connor was the only one he had ever seen left whole for more than a day. Connor absently watched her splash her foot in the puddle of blood. *Whack!* The hatchet hit its mark—exactly an inch to the right of the heart. *She is so precise...* Envy again washed over him. He inched closer to the bars to see how she handled the hatchet—removing it from the chest cavity with a gentle wiggle and plunging it back in, this time exactly an inch from the left wall of the heart.

His first days in the cellar had been waking nightmares. The first of his cellar-mates had had the flesh above his hips burned away by acid. His agony was reflected in her eyes. In those days, Connor had regarded her as a ghoul. Her tiny smile as the boy had screamed had sickened him. He had desperately longed for his foster parents' to come and find him and yet he wasn't surprised when they failed to do so. It was his third day in the cellar when he noticed that she wore a locket around her neck. The chain had gotten caught on her thumb as she swung the axe, which ended the first boy's life. The force of the swing had wrenched the chain, snapping it. The locket had flown off and landed at Connor's feet. Falling had caused the hinges of the locket to spring open. Looking, Connor had seen a family photo inside: a mom, dad, two sisters, and a brother.

Suddenly, Connor realized that she was staring straight at him. She had finessed the hatchet from the flesh and was lovingly fingering the blade as her mirror-like eyes took him in. For the first time in his memory, she spoke:

"Would you like to try?"

Connor felt himself lean forward and glanced eagerly at the hatchet in her hand. Looking up, his eyes met hers.

"Yes."

She smiled. A new kind of smile. She looked...he couldn't name it. It didn't matter. Moments later, he stood beside her. She rested her hands on his arm and back. Guiding his movements. Her cold fingers warmed against his skin. After a few tries he hit his mark—splitting the ribcage. Adrenaline coursed through his veins. He turned to her for approval. The new smile greeted him. She smudged some blood that had splattered on his face. Their eyes met again. He wrapped his arm around her. He pulled her close. Blood pooled at their feet. Now he understood why she never wore shoes.

An hour later the boy in the cage finally breathed his last breath. Connor was looking directly in his eyes.

"Watch the flame go out." She had whispered moments before.

The adrenaline that he had felt earlier resurged. There was something invigorating about inflicting death on another. Something beautiful in the shaping of the corpse—a little off here, a burn there. She joined him, sliding her frosted hands around his waist. She rested her head against his chest and he nestled his chin in her black-brown hair.

In the corner of the cellar sat the skeleton of Looney Luke. Old age and illness had done their work, but not before he had done his. His boney grin showed approval to his created children. His workshop had served its purpose.

October 31, 2003

<u>Evening News</u>: Couple disappears on the bus ride home, leaving behind three foster children...

November 5, 2003

<u>Evening News</u>: Doctors confirm that missing couple abused children in their care! Police suspect they were involved in an underground network, which exploited children in the foster care system...

December 13, 2003

<u>Evening News</u>: Fragments of couple suspected of child abuse and exploitation found throughout Central Valley wheat fields...

The Boxer
✤
Chris "Irish Goat" Knodel

The Boxer (1859)

Yankee Stadium: The Bronx, New York City, NY
Mickey "Toy Bulldog" Walker versus Sean "Red
Rooster" Flannigan
May 28, 1925

Sean stared across the ring. Mickey "Toy Bulldog" Walker looked bigger than last time. More confident. Sean looked down at his gloves. Tonight was his chance. He wouldn't have another. He released the ropes, crossed himself, and exhaled. The bell rang.

Sean ducked Walker's crushing roundhouse and wove to the right. He threw a combination that ended with a forceful uppercut. Walker staggered back, dazed. Sean wanted to keep the advantage. Bulldog was a talented and dangerous fighter. So aggressive, in fact, that the New Jersey Commission suspended his boxing license for a year. The Bulldog was well on his way to the top, to fight solid contenders, like Dempsey, Greb and Malone.

Walker moved in with two body shots and a series of rapid jabs to Sean's ear. The pain shot through him, triggering his anger. Sean blocked the worst of the onslaught, but had trouble breaking free from Bulldog's attack. Two left jabs and a vicious roundhouse right met Sean head-on. And just like that, his rage awakened.

That's how it was with Sean. The anger would start as a smoldering coal. The more damage he received, the more it wafted its heat over him. Then the flames would ignite. He felt it now, as he stared at his opponent. Sean shot forward and pushed him into the corner. The crowd went wild, as Sean released himself to his temper's warm embrace. A right to the face, a right to ear, a right to the face again, and three rabbit punches to the right side.

Sean moved in for the knockout, and remembered the last time he fought Walker. Fourteen months ago, they faced off in Chicago. But this time was different. Sean had taken the pay-off. When Marcel signaled him in the eighth round, he would take the dive. And it was a huge score; his biggest yet. The Italians put all their money on him going down in the eighth. The Irish backed that bet and arranged the fall. Both crews would rake in the cash.

But Sean didn't back down. He knocked Walker out and disappeared. Since that night, he'd been on the run. Fourteen months of hiding. Fourteen months of back-alley fighting and living in the shadows. He'd had it with that life. Tonight, win or lose, it had to end. A jab to the ear brought him back to the present.

"You're nothin'," the Toy Bulldog exclaimed in a thick Jersey accent. "You'll be down before dis round is through. I put down Britton for the title. Yer nobody. Ya hear me? A bum." Walker smiled, and his black mouth guard showed smears of blood.

Sean looked into his eyes. Bulldog was bluffing. He was hurt, and he was worried. Walker was on the downward spiral. The next two rounds were mediocre, with neither fighter pressing their advantage. Each would jab and retreat, attack and withdraw. It was a conservative pugilistic display. The crowd sat down. The shouting became sporadic. To break their silence while his regained his full strength, Sean moved in to rouse the mob.

He danced around Bulldog, throwing fast jabs to his chest and shoulder. None were intended to do much, save engage the audience. Walker watched him showboat; he stayed grounded in the center, blocking what he could of the Red Rooster's display. And with only eighteen seconds left in the round, Bulldog unleashed a furious combination. He threw three explosive rights to the head that left Sean on the mat. He felt his consciousness going, as he watched the incandescent lights swirls above him. Blood filled his right eye. He could hear, as through water, the referee.

1... 2...

Sean fought to get up. He rolled over to his front, on elbows and knees in the center of the ring. The ropes were too far to grab. He had no time to crawl.

3... 4... 5... 6...

Sean saw Bulldog with his hands lifted in conquest, facing the crowd. He rose to one knee. His body rocked back and forth.

7... 8...

Sean pushed off of his knee to stand, weakly. He stumbled towards the ropes as the referee ran to him. Sean waved him off, signaling that he was okay. Walker had already started towards him. He threw up his hands to block. The bell rang. Bulldog kept punching. The ref had to get between them; he had to pull Walker off and lead him to his corner. The crowd had exploded into a raucous din of fist-shakes and blood cries.

Sean slumped down on his stool and toweled off his face. His skin had split above the right eye and was oozing. He hadn't been able to see much since Walker dropped him. Marcel ran up with smelling salts, cut jelly and a cup of water. While Sean drank, Marcel went to work. They had been through this before. A cold towel, eye iron and some petroleum stopped the bleeding. Marcel surveyed his work, and nodded that he was done. Sean stood, and looked out into the crowd. Then he spit the last of his water over the ropes and turned to face the Bulldog.

Marcel leaned in and whispered to Sean, "He's been favoring his left side since you pinned him, *mon ami*."

Sean nodded.

Walker had completely surprised him. He had been overconfident—too cocky, too sure. As the bell to the sixth round rang, Sean rushed out of the corner. He needed to turn the tables or he'd end up going down. He took two jabs to the face in order to get close to Bulldog. Then he landed a forceful right hook to the gut. Walker bent forward as Sean launched an uppercut to his chin. A second crushing belly-blow followed by a roundhouse to the ear opened up his opponent's guard.

Sean pinned him to the corner a second time, but while in close quarters, Bulldog started punching below the belt. Sean felt the bile rise in his throat. Walker threw a fourth and fifth jab into his genitals, as the ref's view was obscured. But the crowd saw the foul, and they went into an absolute frenzy. Sean fed on their energy. The round ended to the din of excitement.

As the bell to the seventh round rang, both fighters rushed out to destroy each other. Walker gained an early advantage, getting several left-handed blows through Sean's guard. Two landed above the right eye, reopening past wounds. A third popped his tender ear, causing him to wince. Bulldog's heart pumped faster; his confidence grew. *He was beating this Paddy!* He saw pain in Sean's eyes. *He was going to win!*

Sean feigned a retreat and lunged forward with his right. He cocked back his fist and looked into Walker's eyes. He punched straight into his face. Again. And again. A thrust to the belly with combinations to the body and head. This was how it was supposed to be. Pummeling enemies and clawing your way to the top of the dung heap. Sean felt his anger peaking. He had pinned Bulldog to the ropes, propping him upright with his body and laying blows one after another.

Walker started dropping his guard. His consciousness was going. Sean punched Bulldog in the stomach and then came up with a final roundhouse. Walker crumpled to the mat. He lay there. The count began.

1... 2...

He didn't move, but his eyes opened. He just looked up at Sean.

3... 4... 5... 6...

Bulldog rolled onto his stomach and drew his right leg in to stand. He grabbed the ropes and pulled.

7...

He collapsed back to the mat.

8... 9... 10.

"You are out!" shouted the referee.

Seven rounds they had battled. Now it was over.

Sean threw up his arms, victorious. His muscles rippled under the sodium lights. His skin was steaming and the vapors mingled with the haze of cigar smoke. He was breathing heavily, even as he felt his rage begin its ebbing flow. His burgundy shorts stuck to sweaty legs, dripping from above the knee. Sean watched the drops splash upon the mat, as he waited for Walker to get up. The referee leaned over him, and the medic knelt down with smelling salts. But the ammonia inhalant didn't rouse him. The knockout had been complete.

Sean was the Welterweight Champion.

Marcel brought in champagne and poured three glasses.

"You did it, Sean," Marcel said while clapping a hand on Sean's back. He felt the sweat through the fabric; Sean's heart was pounding.

"Ma would be proud of you," Jimmy said. "She never watched you fight, but always had me describe the bouts. She loved hearing the stories. You should of seen her smiling while she sewed and rocked in her chair. She tried to hide to hide it, but I always could tell. She'd be so happy."

A knock on the door was followed by a man

poking in his head, apologetically.

"Excuse me, Mr. Flannigan, but would you mind doing an interview for 'The Ring?' We'd love to get your perspective on the match. And a photograph. We can come back later, of course."

"*Non*," said Marcel. "The champ is available now. Come on, Jimmy. Let's give Sean some time with the public. He won't have time later."

Within the hour, they'd be on a streamliner, safe and free. Everything was arranged. They exited the dressing room, leaving Sean with the reporter. The photographer entered and started setting up the equipment, while the interview began.

"So, Mr. Flannigan," he continued, scribbling in his notebook. "How did this fight compare to the one last year? What'd you think of Bulldog? Was it worth not taking the dive?"

Sean heard a revolver cock from behind the camera. The Stetson brim lifted to reveal the stern eyes of Anthony Zito.

"Been a long time, *Champ*," he said. "Wasn't able to get a bead on you and Marcel until you came out for this match. You didn't think we'd forgotten, did you?

He paused and lit up two cigarettes. He offered one to Sean. Sean inhaled deeply.

Anthony took out a flask and unscrewed the cap. He handed it to Sean.

"Head or chest?" Vito asked.

Sean tipped back the flask and drank deeply. Then he looked at the Title Belt, and saw his distorted reflection in the brass. Ma's eyes stared back at him. Maybe the only thing she'd been able to leave him. He knew Jimmy had been right. She would have been proud of him.

He looked defiantly at Vito. "Head," he said, and handed back the flask, empty.

Marcel lay on the concrete floor of the Yankee Stadium shower-room. Water flowed over him, washing the blood into the floor drain. They'd been beaten by men with bats. His spine was broken, his skull fractured. He'd be dead soon. Jimmy's body lay beside him, already cooling. Over the noise of the cascading water, he heard the pistol's shot.

Author Bios

Brenna L. Aldrich: I am a writer, English tutor, and Alumna of the Masters in Professional Writing program at Kennesaw State University. My short fiction has been published at the online magazines *Black Lantern Publishing*, and *LACUNA: A Journal of Historical Fiction*, *The Hoggle Pot,* and is forthcoming in *Hyperpulp*. Though I have written in numerous genres, the heart-line shared by each work is a fascination with characters who confuse, teach, and change me.

Renee Blue is happy to be included in her second anthology. She is from Colorado and has been writing since she was very little. She likes art of all kinds whether it be writing, photography or baking. She hopes you enjoy her story because this is her first attempt at a dystopian tale.

Christa Carmen lives in Westerly, Rhode Island with her fiancé and a beagle who rivals her in stubbornness. Her short fiction has appeared in *Devolution Z Horror Magazine*, *Jitter Press*, *Corner Bar Magazine, Literally Stories, Fiction on the Web*, *The J.J. Outré Review*, *pennyshorts*, the WolfSinger Publications' anthology, *Just Desserts*, and Frith Books' *All Hallows'*. She has a bachelor's degree from the University of Pennsylvania in English and psychology, and a master's degree from Boston College in counseling psychology. Christa works for Pfizer in Clinical Trial Packaging, and at a local hospital as a mental health clinician.

Gene Hines has been a student in Germany, a Marine in Vietnam, a preacher in South Carolina, a missionary in Japan, a legal aid attorney in North Carolina, and a writer in Tennessee. He has won several short story prizes, had one story nominated for a Pushcart Prize, and is a graduate of the Borderlands Press writers' boot camp. Please contact him at bcdejkllmms@gmail.com

Chris 'Irish Goat' Knodel is an author, poet and ultra-distance runner in San Antonio, TX. His poetry and short fiction have been featured in/by *Alba, Allegro Poetry Magazine, Asses of Parnassus, DreamFusion Press, Ealain, Four Parts Press, Glass Lyre Press, Grey Wolfe Publishing, Haiku Journal, Highfield Press, Icarus Down Review, Kind of a Hurricane Press, Pretty Owl Poetry, Tanka Journal, The Wolfian, The Write Place at the Write Time, Writer's Quibble, Yellow Chair Review, Ygdrasil, Zimbell House Publishing, Zodiac Review & Zombie Logic Review.* He can be easily spotted by his kilt, tattoos and six-inch, flaming-red, Van Dyke goatee.

Jason Lairamore is a writer of science fiction, fantasy, and horror who lives in Oklahoma with his beautiful wife and their three monstrously marvelous children. He is a published finalist of the *2012 SQ Mag Annual Contest* and the winner of the *2013 Planetary Stories Flash Fiction Contest*, a third place winner of the *2015 SQ Mag Annual Contest*, and a recent Semi-Finalist in the quarter of *Writers of the Future, Volume 33*. His work is both featured and forthcoming in over 65 publications to include *Perihelion Science Fiction, Stupefying Stories* and *Third Flatiron Publications*, to name a few. You can connect with Jason at Facebook.com/Jason.Lairamore

Sara E. Lundberg is a Kansas-grown writer of the fantasy persuasion who dabbles in everything from horror to haiku. Sara also wrangles the LFK Writers and manages their website, *The Confabulator Cafe*, where they post free fiction they've written every month. When she's not scheming up newer and even more absurd writing-related projects, she watches cooking shows and superhero movies with her husband and stepson while trying to keep her vegetarian pit bull from licking her to death. To follow Sara on her writing journey, visit selundberg.blogspot.com

Bruce H. Markuson is married with two children. He lives in Milwaukee, WI. With abiding faith and diligence he has 100+ short stories published. Bruce is also working on a number of series. He enjoys writing and often finds himself with writer's obsession. He says the best way to write is to have an ending then write to that ending. Check out his blog at brucemarkuson.blogspot.com

A.F. Munson lives in St. Louis Missouri with his beautiful wife and children. He credits God for his talent for writing, and his wife for the patience to love a writer. Aaron has dreamed of sending readers off to strange far away worlds and places, since he first read *The Foundation Series* by Isaac Asimov.

Tina Parmar is an economist who has recently started writing short stories that have an element of horror or surrealism. She got an honorable mention in a *Darker Times* short story competition in the UK.

Joshua Raines: JB Raines is an emerging writer and MFA candidate at Southern New Hampshire University. When he's not writing creepy tales, working on his first novel, or chasing around two small children, he does user experience work for a music education company. The native Texan now lives on the Kansas side of the Kansas City metropolitan area. This is JB's first published work.

S. Rey is the author of a collection of short thrillers, as well as her full-length novel, *A Fine Line*, published in 2014. She resides in the beautiful Rocky Mountains with her husband, James, and their three small children.

Barbara M. Scanlon was born in New York and raised in New Jersey, though she is often told that she is too nice to be a Jersey Girl. She minored in Creative Writing in college and has a Master's degree in English Literature from The College of New Jersey. In 2014, Barbara moved to Colorado and has been enjoying the beauty of that area of the country, though she is still a city girl at heart. In 2015 she became a doting cat-mommy to her furbaby, Niel, who supports her writing efforts by sitting on her feet while she works, preventing her from moving.

Goran Sedlar lives in Croatia, where he wastes his energy reading books, writing stories and sharing his space with two cats and a crazy cat lady. He's been published in places like *Kzine, Typehouse Magazine* and *Literally Stories*.

Douglas James Troxell lives and writes in Macungie, Pennsylvania. He would never, ever leave his wife behind even if she was infected with a deadly disease—because she is much scarier than any disease. His work has previously appeared in *Mobius: The Journal of Social Change, Dark Futures*, and *The Story Shack*. Visit his website at douglasjamestroxell.com

R.M. Warren's fiction has appeared in several publications, including *The Absent Willow Review, The Haunted Traveler, Ghostlight Magazine, Dark Fire Fiction*, and *Quantum Fairy Tales*. He lives in the mountains of Western Maryland with his wife, son, dog and cat. Their 19th Century farmhouse, which over the years has served as a Civil War hospital and funeral home, inspires many of Warren's stories.

www.ingramcontent.com/pod-product-compliance
Lightning Source LLC
Chambersburg PA
CBHW070334260626
47160CB00003B/1044